I0692011

THE MATTER OF THE
PHANTOM
PURLOINERS

WYOMING LAND FLIMFLAM AND
WATER BOONDOGGLE CAPER

STEVE LEVI
MASTER OF THE IMPOSSIBLE CRIME

PUBLICATION
CONSULTANTS
We Believe In The Power Of Authors

PO Box 221974 Anchorage, Alaska 99522-1974
books@publicationconsultants.com, www.publicationconsultants.com

ISBN Number: 978-1-59433-856-4
eBook ISBN Number: 978-1-59433-857-1

Library of Congress Catalog Card Number: 2019933959

The impossible becomes possible
when you understand
the impossible is impossible.

. . . Detective Heinz Noonan

CHAPTER 1

Captain Heinz Noonan, the "Bearded Holmes" of the Sandersonville, North Carolina, Police Department had an inherent dislike of *west*. Not the American West, Wild West, Midwest, Far West, the Northwest, or even the West. Or, for that matter, James West. Just *west*, going *west*. Sandersonville, after all, was the focus of his universe, and the further he got from Sandersonville, the further from home and heart he was. The only exception to this geographic mantra was Alaska, the domicile of his in-laws, where his wife, Lorelei, had grown up. Noonan comforted himself with the belief that Alaska was not *really* west or in the west, northwest, or even the far west. It was in the north, so far in the north that even Alaskans referred to the west, far west, and northwest as the nether parts of civilization—specifically, *the Lower 48, Lower States,* or when they were being particularly derogatory, *Outside*.

Basically, there were three things wrong with the west. First, it was the West. This meant states like Colorado, Montana, Utah, Nevada, Idaho, and the Dakotas. While the Badlands were officially in South Dakota, they stretched, in Noonan's eyes, from the Mississippi River to the Rockies and from the Canadian border to Mexico. There was a very good reason this area was called the Badlands. They were bad when God created them. Bad men forced them to live down their reputation, and in

5

the twenty-first century, oil companies, mining conglomerates, banksters, and fracking keep the legacy of the Wild West—and the Badlands—alive.

Second, wherever you were in the West, you were thousands of miles from salt water. In every direction. Ocean salt water, not the ersatz salt water of the Great Salt Lake. It was not as if Noonan was addicted to *ocean* saltwater air, and specifically, Atlantic saltwater air. It was that he was *not addicted* to sage brush, Gila monsters, and sandstorms. Rattlesnakes, he had more than a passing familiarity, so the serpent population of the West caused him no trepidation. Not so with being more than twenty miles from ocean salt water. From the twenty-first mile and beyond, he got the heebie-jeebies.

Third, the residents of the West did not speak English. At least not the English Noonan was used to hearing. They did not use terms like *blue crab, wahoo, lighthouse, surge, tidal chart, hurricane,* or *firefly* and overused words like *barbeque, corral, lariat, saloon,* and *mustang.* To Noonan, a barbeque was a lowbrow clambake where no clams were baked, a lariat was rope made of hemp not nylon, and a mustang needed a large *M* because it was a classic Ford automobile from the 1960s. He also wondered how cowboy boots could be considered dress shoes, bolos were an appropriate substitute for neckties—one had to be careful with the word *necktie* in the West—and why ten-gallon hats were still called ten-gallon hats if no one used them for bathing.

Then there was Wyoming. It was the last state of the union both alphabetically and in the list of places Noonan had a burning desire to visit. It had twenty-three counties and no major sports team. The state reptile was a horned toad, the state tree was the plains cottonwood, state shrub was the Wyoming big sagebrush, and the official state sport was the rodeo—no surprise there. But then again, state designees were no surprise to Noonan whose home state had an official marsupial, reptile, salamander, dance, insect, horse, boat, dog, beverage, carnivorous plant, frog, fish and even a state pottery birthplace, Seagrove—a misnamed town of 228 on 445 acres. The community was supposed to have been named Seagraves for Edwin G. Seagraves who was responsible for routing the railroad through the community. But the man paid to paint the name of the city ran out of space on the placard, so he dropped the final *s*—and misspelled the *a* as an *o*. North Carolina had a right to have so many state designees—Wyoming, not so much. North Carolina had a population of over ten million. Wyoming only had 585,000, one-twentieth the size of the Tar Heel State, which even had a state toast: the Tar Heel Toast.

When Noonan had been ordered to go to Wyoming, he had mused the state was spelled the way it was to make sure it was always last. "After all, why follow a *W*, the fourth to last letter in the alphabet, with a *Y*, the second to the last letter in the alphabet?" Only later did he learn—from an inflight magazine on his way to the alphabetically last state—the origin of the name was just as convoluted. During the Civil War, a representative from *Ohio* placed the name in a bill for a temporary government in the area that he named Wyoming after the Wyoming Valley in *Pennsylvania* where a battle during the American Revolution was made famous by a *Scottish* poet Thomas Campbell. The proposed, original designation for the territory had been Lincoln, but this name had been rejected. The name "Lincoln" was also rejected for what would become North Dakota. Abraham Lincoln never visited either state. But then again, to be fair, George Washington had never made it as far west as Seattle either.

So why was it, Noonan kept asking himself, that here he was in this charming but remote locale? What moral transgression had he committed causing him to be assigned to this wind-swept community of Washakie? As far as Washakie was concerned, its history was just as convoluted as that of the state. Named for the chief of the Eastern Shoshone, Washakie was the personification of the Native American transition from primeval to civilized (if the United States at any time in its history could be called *civilized*). Washakie – the man—had been born about 1800 to Lost Woman and Crooked Leg. His father had been rescued from slave traders by Weasel Lungs and adopted into Weasel Lungs's family. Washakie's Shoshone birth name was *Pinaquanah*, which translated to English as "Smells of Sugar." He later changed it to "Shoots the Buffalo Running" and, ironically, later still "Gourd Rattler." The name "Gourd Rattler," was a sobriquet because he had a history as a high-stakes gambler renowned for his passion for a Shoshone game of chance involving small stones shaken inside a gourd rattle and then spilled on the ground like dice. The "Gourd Rattler" was historically ironic because at that very moment, descendants of the Shoshone were maneuvering to open a large gambling operation in the general vicinity of Washakie.

To a North Carolinian who knew his state's history began in the 1580s, Washakie was not an historical figure but a contemporary one. Further, while North Carolina was chocked with names of Europeans, the saga of Washakie was replete with true names that could only appear in scholarly publications and be accepted as legitimate. But never on the silver screen. Names like *Fires Black Gun, Large Kidney, Twisted Hand, Four Horns, The Horse, Wolf Dog, Shaved Head,* and *Crooked Leg.* Washakie's claim to fame—and he certainly deserved the fame—began when he headed a large contingent of Shoshone to participate in the Fort Laramie Treaty of 1851. This was a seminal treaty between the United States and representatives of the Cheyenne, Sioux, Arapahoe, Crow, Assiniboine, Manda, Hidatsa, and Arikara nations setting forth territorial claims. Later Washakie joined with General George R. Crook to defeat the Sioux after the massacre of George Armstrong Custer and his 268 men. Washakie was one of the few Native Americans with whom the US government had confidence he would live up to the terms of the treaty. The flipside of the coin was, well, historically speckled.

And why was Captain Heinz Noonan of the Sandersonville, North Carolina, Police Department in this community of 3,582 deep in the entrails of Wyoming? He had been summoned by his reputation as a resolver of unique criminal circumstances. The commissioner of homeland security in Washakie knew his counterpart in Sandersonville as well as Noonan's reputation and prevailed upon the Sandersonville commissioner to "borrow" Noonan for a solution to a unique problem: a transient was under arrest, accused of murdering himself with a weapon that could not be found at a time no one can pinpoint for an unknown motive.

CHAPTER 2

For Sandra Trucco, Wyoming had been a gift for the gods. It was *gods*, she always told herself because she had seen too much misery in her life to use the term *God*. It wasn't that she denied the existence—or the possibility of—*God* in the singular in the Judeo-Christian sense of the term or, for that matter, the generic in the Deistic or Unitarian sense of the term. She doubted the existence of a singular almighty because she had never seen evidence of his work. Or *her* work. The ways of the Lord were mysterious, she was always told, and the only thing she had found to be mysterious was any indication the Lord was working at all.

She had good reason to be skeptical. Her life had not been a bed of roses—was still not a bed of roses. Except if one were to interpret the expression to mean to lie upon colorful bedding only to be scratched unmercifully by a myriad of thorns. She had been born the third child of missionaries—white—on the Blackfoot reservation close enough to the Canadian border that if there was a north wind, you could step out of your hovel in Montana and be blown into Alberta. If the wind was particularly strong, you could end up in Calgary before your next foot came down.

9

Her parents had been parsimonious by circumstance and sanctimonious by choice. Diseased by the twin afflictions, they tried to convince their three daughters wealth was the root of all evil in the world. Two were converted. One became an itinerant Evangelical who spent her winters in Florida. The other was the wife of a Mormon deacon in Kentucky—or was it Tennessee?—who had four children, all of whom were homeschooled and none were ever off public assistance. Sandra had not done the family proud. In fact, neither she nor her family knew where the others were, and no one was spending any time planning a reunion. On her eighteenth birthday, Sandra had hitchhiked into Missoula where she jumped into an empty southbound boxcar. Six months later she was pregnant on the streets of Las Vegas.

Everyone has his or her time of trouble. For most people it is a part and parcel of both the maturing process as well as coming to grips with the hard knocks of the real world, the world in which we *do live* as opposed to the world we always assumed existed. Those who survive and profit from the transition of fantasy to reality maneuver their way to a fruitful existence. And a more profitable one.

If there was any one thing Sandra Trucco learned in Las Vegas, and leaned it quickly, it was the law of large numbers. Things happened because of large numbers, not small ones. On the streets she was individual with no direction of travel. She was living in squalor on a pile of gutted mattress in a tunnel beneath a casino where twenty-five feet above her, billions were being tossed onto gaming tables. She only had to rise those twenty-five feet to become a millionaire.

So, as the expression goes, she got with the program. She traded out an abortion for services at a brothel and slept her way up the illicit industry incline from crib to catwalk to cabaret. Hers was neither a story of doing the best she could with what she had nor the saga of someone tripping into the dark side because of no other choice. She neither loved nor hated her profession; it was just a job. And just like any job, there were edges over which there were precipices from which one would not return. She had a legal compass but not a moral one. Thus, she was selectively stupid, blind, or uninformed as the circumstances required. Because of that eclectic world view, she went places where even the bad girls were not invited.

10

She had inherited her parents' parsimonious ways but for a different end. She religiously banked 10 percent of her earnings in mutual funds managed faraway from Las Vegas. She knew there would come a time when she would have to move on. Her life's theme, in reverse, was the old nursery rhyme, "The Old Gray Mare." The old gray mare was not what she used to be because she kept doing the same thing, year after year. Horses, mules, and Las Vegas lounge lizards do not have a sense of tomorrow; only today. Trucco did not love the Strip. It was where she worked. One day she would be too old to work. Age was an occupational hazard in Las Vegas.

So were drugs.

And alcohol.

It was a day of both sadness and opportunity when the piece of flotsam of Las Vegas ended up on her doorstep. Her past came calling when Karen Hutchinson ended up on Trucco's doorstep. Hutchinson had been advised to seek Trucco's help because Hutchinson's name had previously been Denise Three Trees but had been changed to make her white and Las Vegan. Since Trucco had lived on a reservation, in the eyes of Las Vegans, she had undergone some magic of cultural osmosis and was now Indian—the generic term in those days for people who were not African, white, or Oriental.

Hutchison née Three Trees was a lost cause. She was the jetsam of society, and ethnic origin had nothing whatsoever to do with it. She was the human personification of "The Old Gray Mare." She saw the future as nothing more than "tomorrow," and "tomorrow" was only different than "today" by twenty-four hours. At twenty-five years of age, the nightly mix of alcohol and recreational drugs would burn off by early evening. At thirty-five, there was no burn-off, and at forty Hutchinson née Three Trees was incapable of normal human functions. So she was given the boot from her fleabag residence and ended up with Trucco. It was there or the heating tunnels beneath the casinos.

It was not as if Trucco had a soft spot. She had lived in Las Vegas too long to recognize disaster at a distance. So she did what she could. What the social service agencies routinely do. She plied Hutchison née Three Trees for a family of origin, and the name Nathaniel Three Trees

11

in Washakie, Wyoming, came out of the woodwork of née Three Tree's rotting mind. Trucco reached Nathaniel at his Nimerigar office in the basement of his home.

Nathaniel was looking for a connection to a Las Vegas casino for fifty thousand acres of Indian land he was about to acquire in Wyoming.

Sometimes God—or the gods—works in a mysterious way.

CHAPTER 3

If there was any one thing Noonan had learned from his decades as a resolver of unusual crimes, it was nothing is ever as it seems. What the public fails to understand is 95 percent of all criminal investigations are mundane, routine, and low level. These crimes occur, are quickly solved, and the perpetrators are charged and sentenced. The crimes the public knows about are the ones covered by the news media, the sensational ones. There is no audience thirst for run-of-the-mill transgressions. Speeding and drunk driving arrests are a dime a dozen and only make the press when someone is killed. White-collar criminals are rarely punished even if caught; gamblers and marijuana smokers are routinely channeled through the legal process posthaste, and dealing with the mentally challenged is handled by community patrol even if a petty crime is involved. The smartest criminals are lawyers, and they are rarely caught. Only when there is a chance for a ratings boost does the press get involved. Axe murders are grist for weeks of follow-up. Not so divorces, even messy ones, or devious land deals. The media needs footage, not just something fairish.

Further, the media wants exotic, not the unexplained. The exotic adds spice to the local news. It's unusual and is good for a closing segment. Not so much the unexplained. The unexplained raises a real concern: time.

The media wants the story quick, understandable, and now. There is no "quick, understandable, and now" in the unexplained. The unexplained in the news media is synonymous with a game of monopoly. It just goes on and on and on and on and on and on and on and on.

Noonan checked into the Frank M. Canton Hotel in Washakie still lamenting he was so far west. Noonan knew who Canton was in both Wyoming and Alaskan history and marveled at the irony. Here he was in the only hotel in Washakie to investigate a murder and staying in a hotel named for a man who may have killed as many as ten innocent people. Caching, a term coined in Alaska, his suitcase, he made his way across town to the local constabulary—which was within walking distance because Washakie was so small. It was a pleasant seventy-eight degrees, pleasing if you came from the coast of North Carolina where both the August temperature and humidity ran well into the nineties.

Washakie Police Chief Leonard Standing Bear was more than pleased to see Noonan but a little apologetic. "Thanks for coming, and I hope you don't take offense for the call for assistance coming down the chain of command. I only mentioned the case to the commissioner of homeland security here, and suddenly, you're on your way west."

Noonan flinched slightly when Standing Bear got to the word *west*. "Politics is the same the world over. I'll bet your commissioner said something about making this newsworthy."

"Oh yeah. She wants to see her name in the paper."

"Do you have a paper here in Washakie?"

"It's online, but yeah, we have one. But—and I'm sure your commissioner is the same—she wants the story to break statewide. More homeland security money that way."

"It's the same the whole world over."

Standing Bear looked exactly as his name implied. He was built like a bear, albeit a small one. He might have been all of five feet six inches tall, but it was the same all around. Whether or not he was a weightlifter, he gave the appearance of someone who was a regular at the gym. He might have been all of thirty-five. His hair was jet black—no surprise there with a name like Standing Bear—but his eyes were a steel blue, not so common among Native people anywhere in America. His uniform fit reasonably well for his endomorphic frame. He was wearing those cursed cowboy boots, Noonan noted, but sported neither a tie nor a bolo.

Standing Bear handed Noonan a file as the "Bearded Holmes" settled into a leather chair beside Standing Bear's desk. "OK, give me an overview before I go through this." Noonan shook the file as he opened his briefcase and took out a new notebook and pen.

Standing Bear sighed. "We don't have a lot. This is an unusual case. I'd say it would be unusual for a big city much less for a town as small as Washakie. We don't get murders here, rustling, shoplifting, disturbing the peace, n'nat, yes. Murders, no."

"N'nat?"

"Local expression. Means *and that stuff.*"

"Neat term. I'll remember that. Murders are rare?"

"First one in fifteen years. We get dead bodies, now and again, but not murdered ones."

"You sure this was a murder?"

"That, I have to say, is what I'm hoping you can tell me."

"Tell me in a nutshell whacheva you got."

"Whacheva? Local term out of North Carolina?"

"It works."

"Basically, we had a transient check into the Frank M. Canton Hotel, where you're staying. Not a derelict but maybe a salesman or cross-country traveler. Checked into the hotel for three nights. Paid cash. Gave a name, address, and phone number, which turned out to be false."

"No surprise there."

"Morning of the second day, the maid goes into room, and it is drenched in blood. And I do mean *drenched.* I have never seen that kind of blood, and I worked in slaughterhouse in Cheyenne when I was in college. I mean, there was blood even on the ceiling. "High-velocity blood spatter," that's what the forensic expert from Casper wrote in his report."

"No body?" Noonan asked.

"No body." Standing Bear shook his head. "Then things got really complicated. Mr. George Harrison, that was the name he used when he signed in, appeared. Wanted the key to his room. But he was not the same Mr. George Harrison who had checked in two days earlier."

"Not the same Harrison?"

"Different man. Not even close. Mr. Harrison on Day One was short, maybe five two. Mr. Harrison on Day Three was a foot taller."

"And you know this because?"

"I checked with all the clerks. The one who checked Mr. Harrison Day One remembered he asked if room service would send up a case of diet soda."

"Hmm," Noonan mused. "Sounds like he wanted to be remembered."

"I agree. Particularly since there is a standing billboard in the lobby of the hotel saying, 'No Room Service' because the restaurant next door is open twenty-four seven. We're not big-city folk."

"Did Mr. Harrison Day Three seem surprised when you brought him here?"

"Not so much surprised as irritated. Had a whatta-m-I-doin'-here? attitude."

"Did he have an explanation for the blood?"

"Nope. Clammed up and said he wanted a loyer."

"I'm guessing *loyer* is your local term for an attorney."

"Yup. And that's our term for *yeah*."

"I love the West. Did he get a *loyer*?" Noonan asked, mimicking the word with a Wyoming accent.

"Nope. We don't have that kind of a *loyer* here in town. So we took him to the nearest psychiatric facility. In Casper."

"Did he get a *loyer* in Casper?"

"Public defender."

"What did he tell the public defender?"

"In between his stories of the FBI watching him and going to the Vatican to live with the Pope—and I am not making those stories up—he claimed he had been in Casper at the time of the demise of Mr. Harrison Day One. It checked out. Sort of."

"What does *sort of* mean?"

"It means we can place him in Casper for most of the two days between day one and day three but not all forty-eight hours."

"Did he say he was the Mr. Harrison of day one?"

"Hasn't said zip other than he had been in Casper at such and such a time. Other than that, he's been like a clam."

"You checked out his claim?"

"The police in Casper did. He checked out, sort of."

"Not every hour, I'm guessing."

"Not every hour, so he could have come back."

"Did he have a car?"

"Not that we could find."

"Didn't take the bus?"

"Nope. We know that for sure. We checked with the ticket agent in Casper and looked at security tapes in Casper."

"But you arrested him in Washakie on day three when he tried to check into the Frank M. Canton Hotel?"

"We're not big-city folk, so we're not sure of terms. But we didn't *arrest* him. We couldn't arrest him. That's what the public defender said. We couldn't detain him either. So we advised the PD to have him checked into a mental facility. He did, and that's where he is now. As far as the case here in Washakie is concerned, Mr. Harrison wasn't checking into the Frank M. Canton Hotel. He was asking for the key to *his* room. He said he was already checked in."

"Did he have any ID on him?"

"Fake. Matched the name and address the other Mr. Harrison gave when he checked in."

"Anything in his wallet other than the ID?"

"Not much. A paper with some phone numbers and some business cards with the fake name, address, and phone number."

"Any of the phone numbers check out?"

"Not a single one. Then we did the usual," Standing Bear told Noonan. "Not that murder crime scenes are usual around here. We fingerprinted Mr. Harrison and sent the prints to the state troopers in Cheyenne. We had the State of Wyoming crime lab do the forensics. They took blood samples, found some shoe prints, and dusted where they could. If we're lucky, we'll get a DNA match on the blood."

"Anything pop?"

"Not yet."

"When did all this happen?"

"Murder, if it was a murder, was a week and a day ago. So far, we've got zip. What we have is a person of interest who is in Casper and in a

17

psychiatric facility. *But*, and this is a big *but*, he's not there under court order. Whenever he wants to go, well, we can't legally stop him. He's not under arrest. The best we can do is keep him cool and fed and hope he'll stay put. Other than that, zip."

"Any idea who he is?"

"Not a clue. If we're lucky, his fingerprints will match some on file. We took a DNA sample, but it will take a few weeks to get a match—if there is one to make."

"Shoe size?"

"Too big for the crime scene, if that's what you're asking."

"I was."

"How did the two get to town? No rented car in the parking lot?"

"We did a sweep for out-of-city cars the day after the murder and got nothing. We don't have an airport, 'course, you know that, and no bus came through town the day the supposed deceased checked in. There was a bus three days later, the day the suspect showed up to claim his room, but no one got off the bus in Washakie. Twenty-eight passengers got on in Casper, and all are accounted for."

"How much highway traffic do you get here?"

"That," Standing Bear said with a smile, "takes some explaining. Come over here." He got up and led Noonan to the office window. He pointed to a string of mountains in the distance. "Those are the Grand Tetons in the distance. They're hundreds of miles from here, the fata morgana just makes them look close. Those lower mountains looking like foothills below the Grand Tetons are actually only fifteen miles from here. On the other side of those foothills, the Laramie Mountains, is the interstate. It's packed with cars twenty-four seven. There's a rugged road running the fifteen miles through Cannibal Pass . . ."

"Cannibal Pass?"

"Yeah, sort of. It used to be Washakie Pass in honor of . . ."

"Oh, I know who Washakie was. I read history. But where did the *cannibal* come from?"

Standing Bear gave a shrug of his shoulders. "About ten years ago, a group of activist Natives pressured the government to become a federally recognized tribe. It is a polyglot collection of Natives, in the sense they came from many different tribes but who settled in this area: sort of."

"What do you mean by *sort of*?"

"The answer gets very complicated very fast. There is a lot of federal money for federally recognized tribes, but there are quite a few hoops the Natives must jump through. First, you must have land. There is only one group of Native people who have no land. It's the 13th Native Regional Corporation out of Alaska. It was established by the Alaska Native Land Claims Settlement Act. The federal government basically bought out the Natives in Alaska to get the Trans-Alaska Pipeline built. The Native people of Alaska got about a billion dollars in cash and more than a hundred million acres of land. The money and land were divided up among the Native people of Alaska. Then the Native people formed village and regional corporations."

"Is there a Wyoming point to this story?"

"Absolutely. In 1972, there were a lot of Alaska Natives of all ethnic peoples who were not living in Alaska. You know, Natives married to servicemen. Or servicewomen. Or in the service. Students, adopted children. So they could not get a share of the land in Alaska—land, as in acreage—in the Settlement Act. But they were entitled to the money, so they formed what is called the 13th Regional Corporation. Its shareholders got money but no land. As far as Wyoming is concerned—and this area in particular—a group of Native people in this area applied to be a federally recognized tribe enough though they were not all from the same tribe and had no land. They call themselves the Nimerigar, and their members include Sioux, Arapahoe, Shoshone, and Cheyenne. When the feds balked at recognizing them, they pointed to the 13th Regional Corporation as an example of a polyglot tribe. The feds bought it and recognized them. Then the Nimerigar claimed about one million acres of land," Standing Bear pointed off in the general direction of the mountains, "out there. The feds said *no* but ended up giving them fifty thousand acres. About three years ago. That's not a lot of land in Wyoming. Maybe fifteen miles by twenty miles."

"Sounds like a lot of land to me."

"Well, no offense, but you are from North Carolina. Coastal North Carolina at that. Most of your homes are on, what, a half acre? And those homes have access to water and sewer and electricity and even natural gas in pipes or by delivery. Out here, we've got one hundred thousand square miles of state with six people per square mile. What Wyoming has a lot of is land. The Nimerigar got a piece of land, and that's it. No water, no access roads, no electricity, no sewer lines, no natural gas. They got a load of nothing, just a lot of lizards, rattlesnakes, squirrels, voles, wasps, fleas, and bedbugs."

Standing Bear sang a verse:

> How happy I am when I crawl into bed,
> And the rattlesnake rattles his tail at my head,
> And the gay little centipede void of all fear
> Crawls over my pillow and into my ear.

"That's from 'Starving to Death on my Government Claim.' A lot of homesteaders came to Wyoming—and almost all of them left. What the Nimerigar are trying to do is nothing new. They are just repeating the failure of the homesteader. It was close to impossible to make a living on government land a century and a half ago. It's just the same today. Nothing has changed since the 1870s."

"They can't drill for water?" Noonan was interested, but the expression on his face showed he already knew the answer.

"Oh, they can drill, but there's no water there. The nearest water is Buckle Bunny Lake. But it's quite a ways from the Nimerigar land, maybe fifteen miles. Running a road across someone else's land is legal because it's access. Sucking up water from lake is legal because all water bodies are federal. But it's getting the water from the lake to the property that's the bugaboo. You've got to own that land; you can't just drop a waterline along the ground on someone else's property."

"Buckle Bunny. Nice name."

"You know what a Buckle Bunny is?"

Noonan smiled. "I do my research. It may not have been on the plane coming here, but I did read up on Wyoming. Knew about the Johnson

County War before I came here because Frank M. Canton was a US marshal in Alaska, and my wife is Alaskan. I know about the Fetterman Massacre, jackalope, the two-headed calf in Upton, Death Ship of the Platte River, and, of course, Mother Featherlegs."

"Well, you know a lot more about Wyoming than most of our high-school graduates."

"Is your story going somewhere?"

"You asked about the possibility our victim and the suspect could have come in from the highway. The answer is a strong *yes* if you mean the interstate. Locally, we don't get much traffic. But I need to explain the reasonable possibility that the two Harrisons came from the highway even though the highway is on the other side of those rugged mountains," Standing Bear said pointing into the distance.

"I'm all ears."

"Well, the feds gave the Nimerigar the land, all right. About three years ago. Everyone is just waiting for the actual paperwork to go through. The land is out there." He pointed toward Cannibal Pass again. "At the foot of those mountains. On this side of the mountain range. Only problem: there's nothing there. No water, no road, nothing but badlands. But the Native people—they demand to be called Native people, not Indians— took the land and started talking 'bout a casino."

"So they started building a road from the highway."

"Yup. Sort of. That's when things got complicated. Crossing federal property was not a problem. You just do it. It's not illegal. But a lot of the land the road crossed was owned by some corporation back east, which got the land a century ago. Stole it, actually, with a treaty they never honored with a tribe that no longer exists."

"Do I detect a bit of animosity?

"Oh yeah. That treaty was with my ancestors. But that was a long time ago. Half of me is sympathetic to the Nimerigar because they are fighting for their rights even if it's a century late. The other half of me, and particularly the law-and-order half"—Standing Bear pointed to his badge—"knows that it's just a scam. The promise of jobs at a casino is the bait. When the casino gets built, a few Natives are going to make a lot of money, but most of the Nimerigar are going to get nothing."

"That's the way of the world. Nothing unique to Natives," Noonan said. "It's happening every day in the non-Native world."

"It's called progress; you can't stop it." Standing Bear shook his head sadly.

"What did the corporation owing the land say about the road?"

"This is Wyoming, and nothing is simple here, particularly when it comes to land. As soon as word leaked that a casino might be coming in, a foreign company, the Stupinigi Corporation, bought the land from the eastern conglomerate or whatever it was called. But land ownership is complicated. Not all the roadway the Nimerigar claim is on Stupinigi land. At least that's what we think. No one knows for sure because the land-title documents are based on a-century-and-half-old landmarks that are long gone. So, no one is really sure who owns which acres out there. Like I said, a road on federal land is no problem. As long as you don't cross any critical wildlife habitat or cut through an historical area, the feds don't care. For the land owned by Stupinigi, there was nothing the feds could say. First of all, the road that Nimerigar are calling their own now used to be a wagon trail. The road was already there, so to speak.

Second, the Nimerigar had the land, and you cannot block access to someone else's land. If you mean did the Stupinigi Corporation 'yell and scream'? Nope. Not a peep. Anyway, a road went through, from the interstate over Cannibal Pass all the way into Washakie. It's a typical badlands road, but it is passable. Has snow during the winter, but we're three months from any snow. So, yes, there is a way for someone to get here from the interstate, and I'm guessing that's how our two unknown gentlemen got here. No other reasonable way for them to arrive."

"What about the Cannibal Pass you mentioned?"

"As soon as the Nimerigar got their land, they started renaming things. The passage over the mountains used to be called Washakie Pass. That was the first change. The Nimerigar said Washakie had been a sellout to the white man, so they renamed the pass."

"After themselves."

"Yes. They chose their name, the Nimerigar, from the mythical little people who inhabit the area."

"Every culture has something like that."

"Not like the Nimerigar. They're cannibals. They eat people. Shoot them with poisoned arrows and then eat the dead bodies. That's why the pass from the Interstate is known as Cannibal Pass. The Nimerigar, the Native people, have petitioned the State of Wyoming to officially rename the pass Nimerigar Pass. Until then, we all know it as Cannibal Pass."

"Interesting. Historically, that is. So, there is a road, a way for your victim and the survivor, so to speak, to get to town. And if the victim is not really dead, a way for him to get out of town."

"Unlikely." Standing Bear shook his head. "There was too much blood for him, the victim, that is, to have survived."

"So he's really a victim."

"Appears so. At least that's what the coroner said."

"But you can't charge the suspect because you've got nothing. No body. No motive."

"Correct. Nothing that will stand up in court. We've got no body and no MOM. Suspect has an alibi—of sorts—and no weapon."

"Any indication as to how the body was moved? I mean, a trail of blood out to car, for instance, or a bloody tub where the body was cut up."

"Nope to both of those."

"How about other travelers in town? Other people in the Frank M. Canton Hotel? And the other hotels, motels, bed-and-breakfasts?"

"All checked out. Nothing."

"So far you've done everything I would have done. Let's be creative thinkers."

"How do we do that?"

"We change our perspective. What we have been doing is concentrating on crime that may or may not have been committed. So let's see if there are connections to other incidents. Has anything unusual happened in, say, the week before your victim came to town?"

Standing Bear thought for a moment. "Not really. Nothing unusual."

"Well, what was usual?"

Standing Bear chuckled. "We're a small town, Captain."

"Heinz."

"What?"

"Heinz. I'm not a captain here."

23

"OK, Heinz. I'll be Leonard. You wanted to know about anything unusual before the Harrisons showed up? Hey, we're a small town. Everyone knows everything about everyone. You know, small-town gossip. So, what do you want? I mean, I can tell you all about the widow Smith or the widower Jones. Then there's the autistic child of the Hargreaves and how the State of Wyoming keeps denying them education supplements or the visually impaired in the school district who are being funded in a roundabout manner everyone knows about but no one is reporting. What exactly are you looking for?"

"If I knew that, I'd be the genius everyone says I am."

"Quite a burden, eh?" Standing Bear laughed. "OK, let's try this a different way. I'll give you the rundown of the fed and state action. Then I'll go organization by organization."

Noonan laughed. "Let's try this another way. What have been the big and little newsmakers in the past, oh, six weeks?"

"OK, but there's not much to report. When it comes to the feds, there are a number of projects that are in the process of becoming a reality. These projects include some repaving of the highway and pothole filling before winter and repair of the two Indian elementary schools; some drug-addiction-intervention programs have just been refunded, and there are rumors of an early-education task force to take care of special-education children before they arrive in kindergarten.

With regard to the State of Wyoming, we, the county seat, are in the process of computerizing our land records so they can be online; we are beginning an antipoaching campaign, which has been stalled because of the unclear land-status claims by the Nimerigar; there is a joint state-federal antimarijuana effort underway that is not popular here and is only getting begrudging support because there are advertising dollars involved. The quality of education continues to be a hot topic. Affirmative Action is creating a lot of interracial discussion, and the sport-fishing laws are being revised because of invasive species.

Locally, the ongoing drama—and I use that term purposefully—revolves around the Nimerigar. There is always something popping out of the woodwork. A day does not go by before another new issue pops up. Not in any particular order of occurrence or importance. The Nimerigar are attempting to get their land—which has not been finally conveyed to them—declared as a sovereign territory. They are looking for kind of an Indian-nation designation. Not a reservation, but autonomous entity. It goes without saying that they can establish a gambling casino on the land which has been conveyed to them, but Native courts are something else. Even more important, though it has never been stated publicly, there is concern among law-enforcement people that the Nimerigar want the sovereign-territory status so they can grow, sell, and transport marijuana. Recreational marijuana is currently illegal in Wyoming, but if the Nimerigar get sovereign status, they can grow it on their land, sell it on their land, and presumably load up an airplane and transport it from their land to a state where recreational marijuana is legal—or to a reservation for sale in another state off that reservation."

"Can you grow marijuana around here?" Noonan asked. "I'm betting there is a real reason they call this area the Badlands."

Standing Bear smiled. "You can grow marijuana anywhere; it's just a matter of how much effort you want to put into it. The Badlands could probably support marijuana if you improve the soil. But the big problem isn't soil; it's water. There's no water on the Nimerigar land. I'd say the problem isn't soil or sun; it's water."

"Could you grow enough marijuana on Nimerigar land to be profitable?"

"I have no idea. All I can tell you is the Nimerigar is an activist group whose members believe the land they are going to get will make them wealthy."

"Is there any other way to make money off that land? I mean, other than a casino?"

"I'm not sure they're going to make a lot of money off the casino. To get to the casino from the interstate, you have ten miles of very bad road. To get to the casino from Washakie you've got fifteen miles of very bad road. In between the two you've got lots of nothing. Then there's the building of the casino itself. That's going to take money. A lot of money. Where's the money going to come from? If it comes from another casino, say, in Las Vegas, then the Nimerigar are going to have split profits. That is not going to make anyone in this area happy."

"What's the read on the Nimerigar getting sovereign rights?"

"No one, no fed and no state official, has said they have a chance. First, they do have any historical record as a tribe. Second, there is no problem that will be solved with sovereignty. Juries in this county are ethnically mixed. You can't get an all-white or all-Native jury here. Schools are the same way: ethnically mixed. So what problem would sovereignty solve? If there is no difficulty to be resolved, there is no reason for sovereignty. That's the read I get, but no one, fed or state, is saying it openly."

"Is there any other dispute with the Nimerigar?"

"Just one? No. Many, yeah. They want to restrict hunting on Native land they do not yet own. There is a move to amend state law to allow for mining and fracking on soon-to-be Indian land. There have been discussions with energy companies to establish a solar-power farm on the land. The Nimerigar are trying to get the land, vacant land, designated as farmland so they will be eligible for rural-development moneys from the feds. They have applied for economic-development grants from the state and are applying for federal and state grants for exotic projects. Like I said earlier, it's an ongoing drama."

"How are the residents of Washakie taking it?"

"No one's laughing, but quite a few of us are shaking our heads. White and Native. On one hand, we view the Nimerigar as a group of people trying everything they can think of to make a living. We like that. It's as American as apple pie. On the other hand, they're shotgunning. Better they take one or two projects and see them through."

"Not a lot of help in solving our murder here."

"I didn't think so."

"OK, how about after the murder? Anything unusual happen?"

"Funny you should mention that. Yeah, but I did not see any link to the murder—or whatever it was that happened in the Frank M. Canton Hotel. It happened two days later."

"OK. Don't keep me in suspense."

"First, let me give you a little background. And like I said, I don't see it has anything to do with the murder."

"OK."

"Don't think of Wyoming as a state. Think of it as a small town on a very long street. We've got a very small population scattered over a very large area. We don't look at the next town down the road as a different city the way someone from Sandersonville would look at Durham or Chapel Hill. We look ourselves as all in the same pot of stew. A lot of us are related to people in other communities; we do business along the interstate, and our kids go to high schools with other kids from four or five small towns. We know what goes on in those towns because, well, we're on one long street."

"And you are telling me this because . . ." Noonan let the question hang.

"You don't live here, so you do not understand the connections. We may not know everyone in the surrounding towns, but we do know enough of them personally that news gets passed around. That being said, there have been three robberies in the area which are, how shall I say it, odd."

"Are they connected to the two, maybe, Harrisons?"

"Doubtful. MOM is the same for all robberies. One was in early May. The second was over the Fourth of July weekend, and the latest one was two days after the Harrison matter. But I don't see any connection."

"What makes them odd?"

"What was taken, how much the loot was worth, and the fact that the perps simply vanished."

"Vanished! That seems to happen here quite a bit, don't you think?"

"You're referring to the first Mr. Harrison. But the crooks were a different kind of vanishing. We know what they look like; we just can't find them."

"Someone robbed a business here in Washakie, and you could not find them in a town this small?"

"That's about the size of it."

"Maybe they drove out of town or took the road over Cannibal Pass."

"Nope. We had roadblocks up within ten or fifteen minutes. Had one where the road over Cannibal Pass meets the interstate, and the state troopers backtracked all the way to Washakie. The roadblock on the rural highway, both directions, stopped a fair amount of traffic, but no one fit the description of the perps. One was about six two, and the other five foot and no inches."

"A real Mutt and Jeff team. You sure your witness described them correctly?"

"Got 'em on film. Yeah, the descriptions were correct."

"The same pair on the other robberies?"

"We assume so. We got them on film here. The first two robberies, in Colter and Bridger, all have the same descriptions from the victims."

"Tell me about the robberies."

"I don't know why. They're not connected to the Harrisons."

"Humor me."

"Sure. Your Mutt and Jeff team is composed of a man about six two and a smaller person, possibly a woman, who tops out at five feet. In all three cities, they went after the same victims: a coin store and a jewelry store."

"Both of them at the same time?" Noonan asked and underlined the words *coin* and *jewelry* in his notebook. "I mean, they robbed the coin store and then the jewelry store on the same day or the coin store on one day and the jewelry store the next day?"

"Oh no, the same day. One right after the other. Some binge. Hit the coin store, and while the cops were investigating the coin store robbery, they hit the jewelry store across town."

"Across town? This is Wyoming. Rural Wyoming. How big are Colter and Bridger?"

"Same size as Washakie, give or take."

"So, we are talking, three to four thousand people tops?"

"Give or take."

"So these coin and jewelry stores are small. For locals only. How much was the take?"

"That's what make them so strange. The thieves had guns and did what is basically a smash and grab. Then they walk away with a few thousand dollars. At the most."

"Anything Washakie, Colter, and Bridger have in common—other than the robberies?"

"Sure. They're all small towns in Wyoming."

"C-l-e-v-e-r. Anything else? How far apart are they?"

"As the crow flies, about sixty miles. Each of them. Imagine an equilateral triangle with the three cities as the points."

"Any other similarities."

"Not that I can think of. What I can think of is how different they all are."

"In what way?"

"What does this have to do with the Harrisons?"

"Who knows? I find the Harrison case compelling. But there's a reason it's happening. I'm trying to see if there is any connection to anything else."

"I don't see how it connects, how any of it connects. The robberies are strung out over a four-month period, and the most recent one, the one here, was two days after the surviving Harrison was taken to Casper. So why are we having this conversation?"

Noonan leaned forward and whispered, "Because I love a mystery."

Standing Bear just shook his head and smiled. "You're the boss. Believe it or not, all three towns are historically different. So different when the State of Wyoming was established in 1890 they were put in three separate counties. Bridger was a mining community. It made its money—and its tax base—from hard-rock miners. Over the years, the mines have come and gone."

"What kind of mining?"

"Embarrassingly little, I'm afraid to say. We've never had gold like California and Colorado, but we have enough to keep the small operations going. Then there is some copper and, I think, silver. Got some coal and oil but not much else. We are not talking huge finds here—the reason communities like Bridger stay small. There are enough minerals coming out of the ground to keep the town above snakes, the schools funded, and the police and fire departments small but functional. Bridger is also cattle country. In the old days, cattle could roam free, and every spring there was a roundup. I'm sure you've seen roundups on any one of a hundred cowboy movies."

"They still do roundups?"

"Naw. Everyone's got fences now. Open range is still there, but it's government land, state and federal. Sure, you can graze cattle there, but you have to pay for it. Or not. Remember Cliven Bundy in Nevada? His sin wasn't that his cattle were on federal property. He just didn't pay for the grazing. That's a no-no. Everyone in Wyoming who grazes cattle on state or federal land must pay for it. Ranchers in Wyoming do; Bundy didn't. He was a skinflint. Not a very popular fellow around here."

"I thought you said there wasn't a lot of water up here. Except for Buckle Bunny Lake. Where do the ranchers of Bridger get their water?"

"Buckle Bunny Lake is a good source but not the only one. Bridger has ground water too. It has a water table. Not a lot of water but shallow enough for grass and shrubs the cattle eat. Town itself is on well water."

"OK, how about Colter? Does it get any water from Buckle Bunny Lake?"

"No. Too far. Sixty miles or so. It uses well water too. They do have some rivers in the area. Mostly spring runoff from the snowpack in the mountains. It has a small reservoir that fills to capacity in the spring and then is slowly drained off during the hot months."

"So neither Colter or Bridger have water problems?

"Nope. They have tourist problems. They try to attract travelers from the interstate. Neither Colter nor Bridger is on the interstate. Washakie is not either, but then you know that."

"So the coin and jewelry stores in Colter and Bridger sell to more than locals?"

"Sure. And tourists. But it's not a land-office business."

"But they are making money?"

Standing Bear chuckled. "You city folks. Captain, . . ."

"Heinz."

"Right, Heinz. You are thinking like city folk. Keep in mind there is not a lot of money in these small towns. The coin stores and jewelry stores in Washakie, Colter, and Bridger are not selling their own inventory. They are more consignment shops than sales outlets. When the coins and jewels were stolen, any insurance moneys went to the owners of the coins and jewels. Not the owners of the shop. So even if there were a million dollars in inventory stolen, the coin-store owner and the jeweler would be getting peanuts. If you are thinking there is some kind of an angle where the shop owners are in cahoots with the perps, there is no monetary reason for that to happen."

"Well, you never know what is important."

"You're the expert here. I can put you in touch with the police chiefs in Colter and Bridger if you care to talk to them."

"Yes, I would. I'd also like to talk to locals if you don't mind."

"Just let me know who, and I'll set it up."

"Let's start with the Frank M. Canton Hotel people. Then I'd like to talk to the local banker—you do have a bank here, yes?"

"We're not that much of a frontier, Heinz!" Standing Bear thought that question was worth a laugh.

"You said that the robbery here was taped. Was that right?"

"Sort of. It's on a baby cam."

"A baby cam?" Noonan was surprised, and it showed in his voice.

Standing Bear sort of shrugged his shoulders. "After the two robberies in Colter and Bridger, the coin store and jewelry store here in Washakie took precautions. The coin store installed a baby cam . . ."

"Baby cam. One of those cameras you put in a baby's room to keep an eye on the child?"

"Yup. We're low tech here because no one has the money to be high tech. It's the best the coin shop could do. The jewelry store didn't do much better. It installed a burglar alarm . . ."

"Which didn't do diddly because the robberies were daylight."

"You got it. Welcome to Wyoming thinking." Standing Bear was working on a list of names on a sheet of yellow paper. "Who else do you want to speak with?"

"I'll have some more names as I get deeper into this case but, off the top of my head, in addition to the names you already have, the coin- and jewelry-store owners, the state trooper or troopers who set up the roadblocks, any car-rental agency in town . . ."

"We don't have one."

"How about a bus-ticket agent?"

"I'll do that as well."

"Eventually I am going to want to talk to the suspect Harrison in Casper. Can you make arrangements?"

"Sure. But he's not talking with us, so I doubt he'll talk to you."

"That's OK. I'm a charming fellow."

"Suit yourself."

"I'd also like to speak with someone from the Nimerigar . . ."

That took Standing Bear by surprise. "Really! Why?"

"Just getting the lay of the land."

Standing Bear gave kind of rolled his eyes. "Let me see if I can say this as politely and politically correct as possible. The Nimerigar people are in a different mind zone, so to speak. They are the kind of people who answer your question with a response that makes no sense. When you and I have a conversation, we exchange information. You ask me a question; I give you an answer. You ask another question; you get another answer. With the Nimerigar you ask a question like 'What are you going to do with your land?' and the response will be something along the lines of 'We have fifty thousand acres of Arapahoe and Shoshone blood-drenched soil and the right to be sovereign on those lands' and then finish with a 'What's it to you, white man?'"

"I'd still like to talk to one."

"It won't be hard finding someone who will talk with you, but you will find it hard to figure out what he or she said."

"I have a lot of experience with people like that. I call them in-laws."

Standing Bear thought that was a hoot and, as he was laughing, he pointed to his wedding ring with a gesture that said, "I hear you, brother."

CHAPTER 4

Nathaniel Three Trees, known locally as Old Man Three Trees, was a survivor. A century earlier he would have been the single warrior who fought the cavalry and avoided the inevitable slaughter on the battlefield and the cross-country chase for stragglers. He had grown up in Wyoming when Indians were considered human garbage, served in Vietnam where he was called a Yankee, returned to Washakie where he was a labeled as a damned Indian activist, and stumbled toward the end of his life as a man fighting for remission from Agent Orange.

But Old Man Three Trees never quit. This was not an attribute he had learned *from* Vietnam; it was a philosophy he took *to* Vietnam. He would have made a great high-school football coach because he was never willing to admit defeat. Every Friday's loss was just the excuse to work harder on Monday, Tuesday, Wednesday, and Thursday afternoons. In Vietnam, this attitude endeared him to his squad—but not his superiors. His superiors did not want victories; they were happy if the quagmire would continue seeping until they retired.

Back in Washakie he got his wake-up call. Into everyone's life comes at least one epiphany, a moment when the tide of normality pulls back, and a pathway to the future is revealed through the rubble of reality. But, crudely stated, every epiphany has a shelf life. In the sands of time, it is only there for a heartbeat, and in that moment you must act. If not, the tide rolls back in, and the pathway is obscured.

His epiphany came in two parts: a synchrony of legislation. Rare in human history, when it occurs, the quick are able to profit far beyond their wildest imagination. Together, the sum of the parts far exceeds the value of the whole. Both occurred in 1972. The first was a statute, known generically as Affirmative Action. Basically, it established the principle—and reality—that white males were relegated to a secondary status when it came to any jobs where government dollars were involved. The states followed suit quickly, and suddenly, not being a white male was an asset. The upside was the breaking of the proverbial glass ceiling that had kept qualified minorities from moving up the occupational food chain. The downside of the upside was the broad-brush stroke of making every minority more employable than equally qualified or more qualified white males.

While Old Man Three Trees had always viewed himself as American first and Shoshone second, now there was a financial reason to reverse the word order. There was profit in the exchange. Federal and state dollars were available for opportunities that had never before existed. Suddenly being an aboriginal was profitable *if*—and it was a very big *if*—there were opportunities that matched federal and state grant guidelines. This was a significant stumbling block in the tri-county area. Combining the populations of Washakie, Bridger, and Colter, the Native population was barely in the triple digits. Worse, the Native population was oxymoronic. There were ten major tribes—Arapahoe, Shoshone, Sioux, Bannock, Cheyenne, Comanche, Crow, Kowa, Pawnee, and Ute—whose members had intermarried among themselves along with whites, blacks, Filipinos, Italians, and Hispanics. Complicating the equation, a portion of the so-called Native population was doing financially well and had no desire to upset the applecart of opportunity. Affirmative Action was providing them and their children with a gold-plated opportunity, so they saw no reason to change the dynamics. Third, even if the first two blockades could be leaped, there was no unifying plan of action. A plane in the jungle has no value unless there is landing strip.

Then came the second gift of Esa, Isa, Issa, Ysa, Esha, Eesha, and Isha translated to English as Wolf, the god of creation of the Shoshone, Bannock, and Northern Paiutes: the Alaska Native Land Claims Settlement Act. For the rest of America, it was just a deal.

In the building hysteria of an oil shortage brought about by allegedly greedy Arab oil countries in the early 1970s, the United States took an activist role to increase domestic oil production. Translated, this meant opening the largest, isolated, undeveloped oil field in the United States: Prudhoe Bay. This was not going to be easy. Prudhoe Bay was 850 miles north of the proposed export port on the Gulf of Alaska, which necessitated an 850-mile pipeline to be built.

This was a problem.

A big one.

In 1971, the US government had passed the Alaska Land Claims Settlement Act, which gave the Natives of Alaska $963 million cash and forty-four million acres of land. The $963 million was given in the form of proxies to every human on the planet who could show a blood quantum of at least 25 percent Alaska Native. The Natives would then form village corporations that, in turn, would establish Native Regional Corporations. The Regional Corporations would get the money, and the individual Natives who had authorized the proxies would be shareholders. To receive the moneys, the Alaska Natives agreed not to stop the route of the Trans-Alaska Pipeline.

The money was easy to distribute—the land, not so much. In 1971, no one knew which acres in Alaska belonged to the Natives because such lands had not been selected and conveyed. Further, to quote Alaskan humorist Warren Sitka, the only thing that moves slower than a dog sled in deep snow is a bureaucrat. While the US government agreed to turn over forty-four million acres of land to the Alaska Natives, very few of those acres had been conveyed. But what was of specific interest to Old Man Three Trees was not the act itself but the repercussions. A deleterious downside to the act was the extinguishing of "all aboriginal rights" of the Alaska Native. Then, instantaneously, the federal government allowed the Alaska Natives to have recognized-tribe status, which made them

35

eligible for federal funding. Most specifically, one Native group was able to recreate themselves from scratch.

Suddenly Old Man Three Trees saw opportunity. If an Alaskan Native group could create themselves and get federal land and money, why couldn't a collection of tribal members in Wyoming do the same thing? All it would take would be a lawyer who didn't have a problem pushing the envelope. And, as a matter of fact, he knew one—a one-sixteenth Cherokee lawyer in Philadelphia. He had served with Old Man Three Trees in Vietnam. Even better, he needed the work.

CHAPTER 5

Noonan did not expect to get very much out of the hotel personnel.

He was not disappointed.

He didn't get much.

But it was enjoyable.

The staff knew he was coming, so they were assembled in the lobby of the Frank M. Canton Hotel when he got there. Everyone, that is, except for the woman who had actually checked Harrison Day One into the hotel. She was not at the Frank M. Canton Hotel when Noonan arrived because she was, in the words of the man who had discovered the blood, "up to her eyebrows in manure." Noonan expressed mild shock at the statement until it was made clear that Harriet, the night clerk, was also a "vet midwife"—an occupation Noonan did not know existed.

"We all do double duty here in Washakie," Noonan was told by Ezra, a lanky fellow who looked part Mexican and part sort of a blended European with the visual accent on Portuguese or Greek. "We're a small town, and there is not that much money running around. So we all have more than one job."

"So you all have two part-time jobs?"

"That's city talk," snapped Melinda, the bookkeeper. "In a big city, you have what you call full- and part-time jobs. Out here we've got jobs we call *makin' a living*. It's not like we clock in and clock out. There's a job to do, and we do it. We get paid for it. Sometimes it's regular; other times it's just availability. Slow times, we watch our pennies. Then when the rodeo comes to town, we don't have time to spend those pennies, but we sure make the dollars. Harriet's lucky 'cause she's got a degree in something, so she can help the vet. Pays by the animal, and if there's any one thing we've got plenty of around here, it's animals."

"And raw land," Noonan added.

"You've been listening around town about the Nimerigar." Melinda shook her head. "Some people. Yeah, we've got plenty of badlands. More than enough to go around. They got fifty thousand acres; so be it. Can't do nothing with that land, so I don't know why they want it."

"Anyone else getting that kind of land from the government?" Noonan asked as he jotted down comments in his notebook.

"Why would anyone want that kind of land?" Ezra said. "It's only good for rattlesnakes and wolf spiders."

"Good point," Noonan said and then changed the subject. "Ezra, it is *Ezra*, right?"

"Same name my mother gave me."

"Ezra, you found the bloody room, correct?"

"And it was a sight. I mean there was blood everywheres. On the floor, the walls. There was even some on the ceiling. A lot of blood. So much blood, it made me sick, if you know what I mean."

"I can guess," Noonan said. "Other than blood what else was in the room?"

"Heck, I don't know. I just opened to door and looked in. That's all it took."

"So, you don't know if there was a suitcase or clothes or anything else in the room."

"There wasn't," cut in Melinda. "Nothing. That's what made it so strange. Bed was messed up in the morning, so we did the usual cleaning. Whoever was in there left early. Some wet towels in the shower and toilet paper hangin' from the roll. But no other sign someone had been there. No toiletries. No suitcase. No clothes hung up. Real spooky, if you ask me. Usually it's the other way around. Rodeo comes to town, and you never know what you're gonna find in a room. Muddy spurs in the sink, hair grease on the bedsheets, saddles in the center of the room."

"No rodeo when Mr. Harrison checked in?"

"Nothing happening," Ezra interjected. "Three weeks from the next rodeo and a month from the Fourth of July. We was quiet as a mouse in barn with a herd of cats."

Noonan smiled. "I've never heard that before."

"Made it up myself," Ezra said smiling.

"Good." Noonan allowed a corner of his mouth to pull up in a half grin. "One last question. When you found the bloody room, you just closed the door and stepped back. Correct?"

"Yes, sir. Just pulled the door shut and had Melinda"—he pointed to the elderly woman standing next to him—"call Leonard, er, Chief Standing Bear."

"But you didn't enter the room again?"

"Nope."

"Was there any blood on the outside of the door or on the floor outside the door?"

"You mean on the floor?"

"Yes, on the floor."

"Nope. Just inside the room. The forensic folk asked the same question and sprayed some kind of liquid on the outside of the door and then used a black light to see if there was any blood."

"Was there?"

"Clean as a whistle. We keep the Frank M. Canton that way."

"While this Mr. Harrison was here," Noonan said and looked from Ezra to Melinda, "did anything strange or unusual happen? Loud noises? Arguments?"

"The only thing unusual was that this guy was quiet. Most folks are rowdy. You don't come to Washakie to be quiet. You come to party. Not this guy."

"No phone calls? No cable channel? No room service?"

"Nothing. Just checked in, and that was the last time we saw him."

CHAPTER 6

Nothing in Wyoming is ever as it seems. What you see is not necessarily what you actually see. Many times living in Wyoming is like watching a magic show. What you see is not what is actually happening. The mild-mannered avuncular grandpa next door is not always what he seems, and, in Wyoming, he may be substantially different in reality than in what you see.

As an historical example, a lauded Wyoming mountain man in his day was John Johnson. In fact, he was such a notable character he was photographed with a pantheon of Western heroes in 1883, a group which included—in the *same photograph* taken in Hunters Hot Springs, Montana, in 1883—Wyatt Earp, Butch Cassidy, the Sundance Kid, Judge Leroy Bean, Bat Masterson, and Doc Holliday along with yet-to-be-president of the United States Theodore Roosevelt. No one believes the photo to be authentic, but it has been raising historical eyebrows for more than a century and a half.

Johnson was living a routine life as a mountain man, such as things were in those days, when tragedy struck. In 1847, his Flathead Indian wife was killed by a Crow brave. This enraged Johnson to the point he declared a one-man war against the Crow. Over the next two decades, he hunted down and killed about three hundred Crow warriors and ate their livers. Thus he acquired the sobriquet John "Liver-Eating"Johnson. Johnson was as tough as they come. Once he was selling liquor to his Flathead in-laws, which was illegal, alone in the dead of winter—a foolhardy trip of five hundred miles that would have been exhausting in midsummer. Midway through his journey, he was captured by a party of Blackfeet braves who, undoubtedly ecstatic to get free liquor, decided to double their loot by selling Johnson to the Crow. Johnson was tied with rawhide bonds and dumped in a tepee while the band went to contact the Crow. They left one inexperienced Blackfoot to guard Johnson.

This turned out to be a bad idea.

Johnson slipped free of his rawhide bonds, kicked the guard unconscious, killed the guard with the guard's own knife, scalped the guard, and then cut off the guard's leg.

Why did Johnson cut off the guard's leg?

So he would have something to eat on his two-hundred-mile trek across the frozen badlands to a trapping partner.

Unlike Alferd Packer who was convicted of cannibalism in 1874, Johnson was never charged with a crime. Apparently, whites eating Natives was legal. But not the other way around. Today Alferd Packer lives on as the name of the cafeteria at the University of Colorado Boulder, which offers, among other fares, "*El Canibal* Mexican Specialties."

Darby O'Reilly looked exactly like what someone in his profession should look like. He was a State of Wyoming clerk. Worse, he had to be a documents jack-of-all-trades because Wyoming did not have a lot of money, so O'Reilly had to represent positions that, in a larger state, would be filled by four or five people. He was the land-title clerk, historical-archive-intake interface, Affirmative Action officer, State of Wyoming Education Grant monitor, and State of Wyoming Environmental Protection Officer as well as State of Wyoming land-egress officer for the three counties that lay west of the Laramie Range.

His had been a good job.

For a century.

It was one of paper shuffling. Paperwork came in. It was filed. Someone asked for it. He found it. He copied it. He sent it out. But things were changing. Now the State of Wyoming wanted everything on computer.

That meant formalizing 150 years of convoluted legal paperwork into a cohesive collection that was user friendly. Hey! That was his job! To be user friendly. That had been the job of the man before him and the man before him all the way to statehood—and territoryhood before that. This progression of men had been friendly, knowledgeable, and, to use a newfangled term, user friendly. Now some computer was going to come along and spoil it all. Why, if everything was easy to find online, another newfangled term, why did anyone need him?

His had been a routine State of Wyoming position for years. Nothing had really changed over the years. This was, after all, Wyoming, and things just pretty much stayed the same. People and businesses came and went, but the problems were all the same, just different faces on the same difficulties. Ownership of the gold mines changed, but it was still gold coming out of the Laramie Mountains. Wyoming was the largest coal producer in the United States—not West Virginia as many Americans believe—and there were a myriad of EPA regulations to learn and follow. Then there were the proposed and actual land-use plans; permission to cross state land; joint State of Wyoming and Corps of Engineers wetlands permits to be monitored; and now, the most hair-pulling-out, the transfer of fifty thousand acres of land to a recently formed polyglot Native association/corporation/nonprofit, which spread across three county lines.

O'Reilly had a real fear of the future. Working for the State of Wyoming was all he knew. He smelled the future, and it was a stink. Computerization was a way of getting rid of employees, not lessening their burden. He knew every one of the bureaucrats up the administrative food chain. All they were concerned about was their job. The rest of the departments be damned. If someone had to go to pay for the computerization, it would not be them. It would be him.

O'Reilly had no illusions of retirement. He would be making half of what he was today with nothing to do all day long, all week long, all month long, all year long. He was tired of the Badlands snow and sandstorms but did not have a plan B. It wasn't that he hungered for the tropics or to retire to a little grass shack in Hawaii. He was not drawn anywhere. He was just driven to go, leave Cheyenne, Wyoming, and the Badlands. He had spent his entire life in a dull job and had nothing to show for it. He had never been anywhere, had no one special in his life. He was Wyoming wallpaper, always there, always dull, never changing, just getting older and older and fading as the year passed.

He wanted an adventure.

He wanted to be gone.

With the coming of computerization, he would be gone. But where could he go? He didn't want to spend the rest of his life slogging the streets of Cheyenne with nothing to do. Somewhere out there was an adventure just waiting for him.

But could he find it?

CHAPTER 7

Harriet was exactly the kind of a matron Noonan expected to find in the Badlands. She was a no-nonsense individual who knew exactly what she was doing. Lanky from years of hard work on the prairie, she was still wearing what Noonan would describe as a smock that had stains he took for blood. Harriet towered over Noonan, and he was two inches over six feet. She had shoes more like boats than boots, and her hands were gnarled with the kind of knuckles a cowboy would have earned from years of ranch work.

While Harriet may have been a sight for sore eyes, she was a steely-eyed professional.

"I pegged Mr. Harrison for a man on the run," she told Noonan. "No luggage, paid in cash, had a hard time writing his contact information in the log." She pointed at the logbook on the hotel counter. "Asked a stupid question, which I figured he did so I'd remember him." Again, she pointed at the counter. Behind the cottonwood slab was a large sign that read "NO ROOM SERVICES. CANTON RESTAURANT OPEN 24/7."

"If this is the Frank M. Canton Hotel and the restaurant attached to the hotel is the Canton Restaurant, why can't you get room service?"

"Family feud," sniffed Harriet. "They're still fighting over the kids. Ownership of the hotel and restaurant will come next."

Noonan smiled. "Same as the rest of the world."

"Just because we live on the badlands does not mean we get along with each other any better than city folks," she snapped.

"OK," Noonan shook his head. "Tell me about Mr. Harrison. Was he unusual?"

"We don't have usual guests here, Mr. . . ."

"Heinz."

"Mr. Heinz."

"No. Just Heinz. That's my first name."

"We don't have usual guests here, Heinz. We're not on the interstate, so we get the slow traffic. A Greyhound every other day, but no one gets on or off. We're just a pit stop. The only time we see a lot of folks is Fourth of July, rodeo weekends . . . got a balloon festival nearly every year, a rattlesnake roundup, and a few others. Get a lot of folks over Thanksgiving and Christmas, but they're linked to locals."

"You said you thought he was a man on the run. Anything about him strike you as odd?"

"Just everything. He came walking it. No car. No luggage. No credit cards. Paid in old bills, twenties mostly. No fifties or hundreds. Really nervous and then asked that dumb question. He wanted to be noticed. No telling why."

"Did he ever go to the restaurant?"

"Not as far as I know. I checked when he ended up dead."

"You sure he's dead?" Noonan was puzzled how she'd know if Harrison was deceased.

"Can't lose that much blood and live. If he's lost that much blood, he's dead."

"Well, where's the body?"

"Wrapped in plastic and dragged out. There's only one of me at night. It would be easy to drag a body out the back door. He wasn't a big man. Angle a car correctly, and you could pull him down the hallway."

"But he didn't have a car."

"The killer might have. How else would the body have gotten out of the room?"

Noonan shook his head. "I was hoping you could tell me?"

"If I knew, I could be a cop," Harriet said snidely. Then she added, "Or one heck of a magician."

45

CHAPTER 8

Though he had lived his entire life in Cheyenne, Darby O'Reilly had never met an Indian. Or, as some of them like to be called, Indigenous people, Native people, or Native Americans. He had certainly seen them on the streets of Cheyenne, all twenty-seven of them. Streets, not Native Americans. Streets he frequented, not all the streets in Cheyenne. But then again, O'Reilly was not the adventurous sort. He didn't have a good idea of a good time because he had never had one. He had been born in Cheyenne in a home where *Leave It to Beaver* was an exotic television program. His mother was a housewife and Methodist Church volunteer. His father worked for the State of Wyoming in the documents department, the forerunner of the department where O'Reilly now worked.

In the same job his father had held.

In the same office his father had occupied.

For the thirty years before his father had died.

Now O'Reilly had been there for twenty-five years.

O'Reilly knew what he had.

Which was blah.

He desperately needed a change, but he could not afford it. Did not know how to get it. All he knew was he had been sitting in the same chair in the same office doing the same job as his father, and his life could be summed up in three windows: the front window of his parents' house he had inherited after they'd died and the two windows of his office, front and back. All three windows revealed a street. O'Reilly didn't even own a car. He had four sets of work clothes, all the same color; a dozen shirts, all white; and two dozen ties, all a variety of blue, gray, and black in solid colors. He had never had a girlfriend or taken a vacation. He had a drinking problem once. Six beers.

What he needed was an adventure!

But needing an adventure and paying for it were two different things.

Then, one day, the fetus of an idea plopped onto his desk. The headache of his existence one month and three years earlier had transubstantiated into an embryo. It had come in the form of the New York Photovoltaic Corporation. It was one of those businesses that only comes into existence because there is grant money available. The US government was taking a swat at solar power, and there was federal money for start-up operations. The New York Photovoltaic Corporation had a development grant and was looking at Wyoming as a base of operation for a number of reasons. First—and O'Reilly suspected most likely—was because the federal auditors were going to be located in New York and Washington, DC, not Wyoming. Distance had a tendency to reduce oversight.

Second, the land required for a photovoltaic operation was small, and there were few places in the United States where acreages of any size were available at minimal cost. But there was a reason land in Wyoming was so cheap. It had no value. If there wasn't water on it, mineral under it, or a stunning view from it, the acres were just home to lizards, snakes, scorpions, wolf spiders, and jackrabbits along with a few coyotes howling at the moon. Worse, from a business point of view, even if the land could be acquired for a song, most likely a dirge, it was still a long way from users of the electric power. While it was easy to collect power from the sun, the loss of that power during transmission was as high as 15 percent. The further the power had to go, the less there was at the other end of the line. Anywhere in Wyoming was a long way from somewhere you could sell power. And if the cost of photovoltaic power was greater than that of coal, there was not much use in building the facility.

However, the concept had a singular advantage: it was on the inside track for federal-grant funding. What this meant was the up-front power-plant cost would be free. The feds would pay for the initial plant and transmission wiring. That made the cost of the first kilowatt of power produced just overhead, a fraction of what a coal-powered-generator kilowatt would have to charge.

Thus, it was a typical New York scam. That is to say, it was the type of scam that was both timeless and geographically appealing, and only within the last three centuries had it acquired the *New York scam* sobriquet. It required brains, balls, and balderdash. It was the same the whole world over. In fact, there was a very good chance that someday an archeologist would discover an Egyptian tomb artwork of a bridge and the hieroglyphics would read "When the pharaoh gives us a development grant, we'll get the deed to both sides of the river from the Hittites and construction money from the Assyrians. We will make a fortune!"

At first there had been great enthusiasm for Wyoming in New York—or, rather, enthusiasm in New York for the possibilities in Wyoming—when the Nimerigar were rumored to be receiving their land patent. The enthusiasm was multiplied one-hundred-fold when it was rumored that the Nimerigar were trying to build a casino. Casinos needed power, and if there was any one thing the Nimerigar land did not have, it was power. Photovoltaics were a viable option but a vain hope. The fifty thousand acres owned by the Nimerigar was certainly big enough for a photovoltaic plant in a remote corner, but the cost was astronomical. The Agua Caliente Solar Project in Yuma County, Arizona, only covered twenty-four hundred acres, but it cost $1.8 billion to build, and the power being produced was so astronomically large that casino usage would just be a drop in the bucket. To be truly economically viable, the photovoltaic project would need multiple casinos on the Nimerigar acreage along with transmission corridors to Washakie, Colter, and Bridger, and beyond those communities to the Wyoming power grid. But those transmission corridors would have to cross federal land—which was doable—and private land, which was not so much so.

But the New York Photovoltaic Company was not without persuasive enticement. O'Reilly was hardly on the path to becoming a millionaire much less a one-hundred-thousand-aire, so if he could "make things happen" for the New York Photovoltaic Company by approaching the Nimerigar about power possibilities, "there would be something in his Christmas stocking," which would make him very happy. O'Reilly didn't see anything that could be done, but since the New York Photovoltaic Company offered him "a paid vacation in Bridger" for a week—while he was on sick leave with the State of Wyoming—he decided to take the trip.

In Bridger, he met Sandra Trucco, and she turned out to be the adventure for which he had hungered. Trucco needed him to complete her enterprise. O'Reilly needed her for sex. For her, sex was a job. For him, sex was an adventure. For both, it was an escape hatch.

Whoever said that the gods did not work in mysterious ways?

CHAPTER 9

Sylvester Hernandez of Washakie Savings and Loan was just as worldly as Harriet and just as puzzled as to the happenings at the Frank M. Canton Hotel.

"At the risk of appearing rude, Mr. . . ." Hernandez had to adjust his glasses to read the small print on Noonan's card.

"Noonan. But Heinz is fine."

"Noonan. Mr. Noonan, I understand you are in town to see what happened to the man what got murdered over in the Canton Hotel."

"That's right."

"Then why are you here? That man had nothing to do with the bank."

Noonan sighed. "It's been my experience that anything strange has to do with money. Sooner or later it comes down to cash. So I thought I'd put a peg in that hole early."

"Well, I can't tell you anything because I don't know anything. I know there was a murder, and that's it."

"Any one open any accounts lately?"

"Sure. All the time. All local people. No one from out of the city."

"How about wire transfers?"

"No unusual ones. It's been business as usual for the past several weeks."

"How about before that?"

"Nothing."

"Since the death of Mr. Harrison?"

"Was that his name? I just knew someone got killed."

"As far as we know, it was Harrison. Any unusual transactions after he was killed?"

"I would not call them unusual, but we had a flurry of transactions a couple of days after Mr. Harrison was killed. You know we had a couple of robberies."

"So I've heard."

"We, that is, the bank had to handle the financial end of the matter."

"What end was that?"

"The coins and jewels that were stolen were insured by the coin and jewelry store. We handled the paperwork."

"Is that something you do regularly?"

"No. But this is a small town. We all step in to help. Harry and Sam have been here since dirt, and neither of them is very good at numbers."

"But they run stores."

"Consignment shops. Not stores. They are small and somewhat profitable. But they do not require a lot of bookkeeping. The robberies took about sixty items, and we handled the paperwork."

"I take it Harry and Sam are the ones who got robbed. Which one was the coin-shop owner?"

"Harry. He'll talk your leg off. Sam's his brother. Quiet as a mouse."

"How much was taken?"

"Don't know. Coins and jewelry don't have hard-dollar values. Total value, no idea. The insurance checks totaled twelve thousand five something dollars. Not much."

"You are right. Not a lot for a robbery." Noonan paused for a moment. "Is that a lot for a town this size?"

"For this town, about right. You have to remember we're not on the interstate. We're back roads here. So twelve thousand five is not bad. But it's peanuts in Casper or Cheyenne."

"Anything big time here. I mean, money-wise?"

"Feds and the State of Wyoming are big. Hire a lot of people and spend a lot of money."

"No other big money? I thought you were getting a casino."

Hernandez gave a hearty laugh. "Pie in the mother-loving sky. Ever since the Nimerigar kind of, sort of, got their land, they've been strutting like prairie chickens. They'll get the land 'cause there's nothing there."

"Could there be something there?"

"Naw. Doubt it. See, to get people to come off the interstate, it's going to take a full-fledged road. All fifteen miles of it from the interstate. That won't happen because the private land they have to cross is owned by a big corporation. Putting in an access road is legal. But a legal access road is no more than two ruts wide. If the Nimerigar want traffic—and they are going to need a lot of it—that road's got to be at least two lanes wide. And paved. The feds and the state are not going to pay for it either. The road's on private property. That's just the road. Then they have to find water somewhere out there. And power."

"You sound skeptical they can do it."

"I'm not skeptical! I'm realistic I'm a nuts-and-bolts person. Just to get started building the casino, you've got to have a road wide enough and strong enough to handle the heavy equipment needed to build the casino. I'm talking cats and road graders and steam shovels and cement trucks and cranes. The building of the road is not going to be as easy as just laying down blacktop. You've got state and federal environmental regulations, and if the feds don't like you, it will be a cold day in Hades before you get a permit. Then you have to convince the feds to have an off-ramp on the interstate, which will not be cheap. Since the road will have to be private, there are security concerns, and weather concerns. You are going to need round-the-clock patrols to make sure nothing breaks down. Then there are the gully washers in the fall and snowdrifts in the winter. Then, if the casino is built, it is going to need a large parking lot and a gas station and bus pullouts. Then it needs paved space for Winnebagos and trailers. And I haven't even started to talk about water and power."

"So a casino doesn't sound positive."

"I wouldn't bet on it."

"I've also heard that there is the possibility of growing marijuana on that land."

Hernandez laughed. "You must have been smoking some of that locoweed. Come on. First, even if it were possible, by the time the crop is harvested, twenty other states will have legalized the weed. Second, this is desert land, the Badlands. It wasn't good for the homesteaders one hundred years ago; what's changed to make the land growable for marijuana? Then, again, there's the question of water. No water, nothing grows."

"So no big money coming from the Nimerigar?"

"Don't get me wrong. I don't dislike the Nimerigar. They're trying to make a buck. I applaud that. But I think they're doing the right thing the wrong way. I don't know what the right way is but trying to turn fifty thousand acres of sagebrush into a gold mine just isn't going to happen."

"Is there any way of making the big bucks here? I mean, is there any idea that's been tossed around for years and just never been tried?"

"Heinz"—Hernandez looked at Noonan's card to make sure he had the name right—"Heinz, we may be small town, but we are not stupid. We have been trying everything to get money into this community. Someone here has tried everything you can think of—and a lot of ideas you would never have imagined, like rattlesnake ranching. Everything that could have worked is working, but it's small. Even the robberies are small. The combined take from the coin and jewelry store, like I told you, was twelve thousand five. That's six thousand per store. And not a dime of that went in Harry's or Sam's pocket."

CHAPTER 10

One should always be cautious of one's partners. Particularly if one is from Wyoming, a state whose history is replete with flimflammers, double-crossers, scam artists, disreputable lawyers, and bandits. A good Wyoming example is Mother Featherlegs. Mother Featherlegs was a madam and saloon owner near Lusk, Wyoming—a community, in her case, one letter away from the mainspring of her profession. She was known as *featherlegs* because she favored ruffled red pantalets that fluttered when she walked or flapped when she rode a horse. Mother Featherlegs was intimate with a local outlaw "Dangerous Dick Davis the Terrapin" and hid the loot and jewelry from his robberies in her brothel. Her luck ran out in 1879 when her body was discovered in the Badlands with moccasin prints of "Dangerous Dick" all about the corpse. "Dangerous Dick Davis the Terrapin" could not be immediately located, as he had absconded to Louisiana with all the money and jewelry known to have been in the possession of Mother Featherlegs. "Dangerous Dick Davis the Terrapin" did not give up his dangerous ways, and several years later he had a date with a hemp noose. Before he left this earth, he admitted to the murder of Mother Featherlegs. He said her name had been Charlotte Shepard, which, it was later discovered, was actually a name in a poem.

So no one knew the true name of Mother Featherlegs.

To this day.

But that's how she is listed on the only tombstone in the United States to a prostitute—erected in 1964.

Joshua Three Trees and the Philadelphia lawyer had been cut from the same bolt of cloth. Three Trees was of the next generation after Vietnam, the generation of greed. No war had tempered his world view, and he had come of age in a day when it was the amount of money you made that was important, not how you made it. Had it been filmed in his formative years, *The Wolf of Wall Street* would have been his role model. He had taken in skepticism of the government with his mother's milk. His life's driving force was one of cash, not conscience. A high-school dropout, he had failed at every job he had tried. Counseling, tutoring, interning, and mentoring had not made a dent in his intellect or world view.

Quite the reverse.

He came to view the world as hostile because he believed himself to be more capable than anyone else, and the reason he was *not* successful was because the whites had all the jobs. The fact his Indian school compeers had gone on to lucrative careers because they were educated did not alter his world view.

Three Trees had never heard of Caerus, the Greek god of opportunity. Fleet of foot because he was winged, Caerus would rush by mortals, the embodiment of opportunity being fleeting. But there was a chance to catch both Caerus and good luck. Caerus had a single long lock of hair that hung from his forehead. If you could snatch that lock of hair as he ran by, you would have snagged opportunity out of thin air. Three Trees was able to grab the lock of Caerus's hair the day his father was buried.

Caerus came in the form of a Philadelphia lawyer who was one-sixteenth Cherokee blood, one-fourth blue blood and 4/4th bad blood. He was the embodiment of every lawyer joke. Old Man Three Trees had known exactly what kind of a lawyer he was. Had read his personality like a book when they had served together in Vietnam. Being a man of the world, Old Man Three Trees knew life in Wyoming was a crooked poker game. When one is in a crooked poker game, one cheats. Just like everyone else in the poker game. To cheat big time, you needed a lawyer. One with an adjustable moral compass.

He knew one.

But for Old Man Three Trees time ran out. All he could do before Agent Orange ate him alive from the inside out was form the superstructure of profit. The old man had created the Nimerigar from thin air. He had converted fifty thousand acres of worthless government badlands into fifty thousand acres of Nimerigar badlands. It would be up to the next generation to take the next step.

Joshua Three Trees met the Philadelphia lawyer in a hotel room after the funeral. It had been the first time the lawyer had made it this far west. The lawyer had made it clear. What the Nimerigar had was fifty thousand acres of garbage. The dreams of a casino were on life support. The only access to the interstate was a wagon rut; there was no water table, and for the photovoltaic deal to go through, there had to be access to the Wyoming power grid.

So the Nimerigar had nothing?

"Not exactly," the lawyer told Three Trees. "There are some possibilities but . . ." and he let the sentence hang.

Joshua Three Trees was no fool.

He nodded, and the deal was cut—without Three Trees even knowing what he was getting himself into.

But then again, he had nothing to lose.

When Old Man Three Trees had died, Joshua Three Trees had lost a place to live and board, cable television, cell phone, and car insurance.

CHAPTER 11

The bus-station manager, ticket agent, and janitor met Noonan with a handshake just as he, Noonan, entered the terminal "Everybody in town's been talking about you, Heinz."

"Bad new travels fast, I see."

"Nope. This is Washakie. We're a small town, and everyone knows everyone else's business. And talk about a mystery! A man who never was, being killed in a locked room, and the suspect is himself with an alibi. How delicious! Anticipating your questions, nope. Neither of the two men, victim or suspect—or one and the same—came in or out by bus. I went back a week before the murder, and six buses came through. All six buses had passengers who got off for coffee, doughnuts, sandwiches, or to use the excellent facilities here." He pointed to a sign reading RESTROOM in the form of an arrow. "No one got off and stayed off. I checked the records and with the drivers. A total of forty-five people came through. And I do mean came through."

"I applaud your diligence. Now, let me ask you a question. How did either—or both—of the men come in?"

"I don't know. What I can tell you is that they did not come by bus. If they came in a rented car, it's not only well hidden but it also wasn't

57

rented in Casper, Cheyenne, Colter, or Bridger. The victim might have been dropped off in a rented car by the survivor, so to speak, and then the survivor came back later."

Noonan flipped open his notebook and started to write.

"But he didn't come by bus, did he?"

"Nope."

"And if he came by rented car, the car's nowhere to be found?"

"Correct."

"So, he had to have been dropped off by someone driving down the highway?"

"Or come over from Cannibal Pass."

"What do you think?"

"I think it's a great mystery. I wish I was a mystery writer. This one would sell and sell and sell."

Noonan thought for a moment. "Any chance the supposed victim is still in town?"

This took the bus-station manager, ticket agent, and janitor by surprise.

"But he's dead!"

"Maybe. Maybe not. All anyone knows at this point is that a lot of blood was found in a hotel room. There has been no body found. So, where's the body? An obvious answer is the individual is not dead, and the blood is simply a distraction. This means that the individual is alive and hiding. Or the individual is dead, and the body is in hiding. But you cannot hide a dead body very long before it starts to, shall we say, deteriorate and send off . . ."

At this point the bus-station manager, ticket agent, and janitor turned a shade of green.

"I see your point. But if there was someone hiding in town, everyone would know about it. After all, we are a small town. On top of that, Leonard, er, Chief Standing Bear and four other officers did a thorough search of the city. The chief is very good at his job. Doesn't leave a stone unturned. Besides that, we had a robbery about two days after the murder, and there was *another* search of Washakie. Nothing turned up there either."

"I heard about the robbery. You're sure the robbers didn't catch a bus out of town?"

"Nope. Checked on that too for Leonard, er, Chief Standing Bear. Six buses passed through Washakie the day of the robbery, and three days later. A family of four—who I happen to know—got off the bus from Colter. No one else." Noonan started to speak, but the bus-station manager, ticket agent, and janitor cut him off, "And no one got on any bus."

"The description of those robbers was pretty specific. Where do you think they are?"

"Oh, that's easy. They went out over Cannibal Pass."

This surprised Noonan. "Why do you think that?"

"No other reasonable way out of town. Roadblocks on the rural highway both directions and a search of the town. They didn't drive out, and they weren't in town. They're on the dodge, and the only place for them to be hiding out is somewhere along the Cannibal Pass road. The cops had the exit blocked on the interstate, but there's lots of places to hide in the Badlands."

"You think they're still there?"

"Well, they ain't here."

CHAPTER 12

Nothing in life is simple. Even something as mundane as replacing a washer on a dripping toilet tank. No matter how easy a YouTube video makes it appear, the actual work is major undertaking involving tools you do not have, strength you have not acquired, parts not available, and a wife who keeps asking "Is it done yet?"

This project had a lot of moving parts. It also had a timetable that was set in stone. This was not going to be a simple undertaking, but then again, it would be very profitable. The two of them would walk away with $2 million apiece. Everyone else would get a lot more. It would take a while for the truth to out, but by the time it did, everyone with greasy fingers would be long gone.

So far everything had gone according to plan. Even the outside investigator. The Philadelphia lawyer had expected an outsider, most likely someone from the FBI. He would have preferred an FBI agent. FBI agents were predictable. They were also closemouthed. You never knew what they were doing. Better yet, they took a long time to make an arrest. In this case, delay was the greatest of all blessings of the FBI. As far as he was concerned, all the two needed was time. By the time the FBI and that outside investigator put the pieces together, everyone involved would be in the wind. Then it wouldn't make any difference what anyone knew and when they knew it.

CHAPTER 13

Harold Standbow—who was German-Irish by ethnicity rather than Shoshone, Arapaho, or Sioux—was quick to point out his heritage to Noonan. "In a department run by a Standing Bear, when you have a name like Standbow, everyone thinks you're Native American. Sometimes it's good; sometimes it's bad."

"Cops are cops," Noonan said. "Once you put on the uniform, you are one of the men and women in blue. You don't have ethnicity."

"That's easy to say"—he paused—"but some folks don't look at it that way."

"There's one in every crowd. I'm . . ."

"Heinz Noonan, the 'Bearded Holmes' for the Sandersonville, North Carolina, Police Department. You want to be called *Heinz*, and you have a passel of questions about the murder of Harrison, the robberies of the Bodacious brothers, and if there's a link to the Nimerigar."

"That's quite a mouthful."

"We're a small town."

"Then I don't have to worry about the niceties of introducing myself," Noonan said as he pulled out his notebook.

"Cop to cop, nope. As far as Harrison, the first one, the professional answer to your question is in three parts."

"Three parts?"

"I like to be thorough."

"Please proceed."

Standbow smiled. "I'm not being rude, just efficient. We're, that is, we in Washakie don't want to waste time. I apologize if I seemed abrupt."

"Not a problem. I don't want to appear nosey just because I am."

That cut a bit of the ice. Standbow smiled and extended his hand to Noonan. "I should have done this first."

Noonan shook his hand. "That makes two of us."

"OK," Standbow continued. "The discussion of the murder has three parts. First, what we did, that is, the Washakie Police Department. Second, what the forensic person out of Casper did, and third, what's happened since. As far as what the Washakie Police Department did, the answer is close to nothing. We responded to a possible murder, opened the door to Harrison's room, closed it, and called the State of Wyoming's forensic people. It did not take a brain surgeon to know we were out of our league. We could have processed the crime scene if we'd had the equipment needed, but we don't, so we called for help."

"Good decision."

"Yes and no. Yes, it is a good idea to ask for help when you need it. No, you look incompetent when you say you don't know what's going on in a murder investigation in a town this size."

"It all works out in the end. Were you the one who went to the hotel room?"

"There were two of us there. I don't remember which one of us opened the door, but we shut it pretty quick. We didn't go in."

"Smart choice. When you were in front of the door, did you see anything like a trail of blood, drag marks or footprints?"

"We answered all of those questions with the forensic people. No, no, and no. Which is very odd, if you ask me. You have a room coated with blood and no sign of anyone leaving the room. I was told—told because I did not see them—there were bloody footprints in the room. Well, if so, why no bloody footprints *outside* the room."

"Good question. Are you sure there weren't and that they hadn't been cleaned up?

"I was there when the forensic people used luminol. No blood, no bleach stains."

"Was there a window in the room? My room at the Frank M. Canton has a window."

"Yup. The window does open, and the forensic people sprayed luminol on the sill, inside and out. Nothing. No scratch marks on the window, inside or out. No footprints of any kind on the soil outside the window. I checked the room of the hotel immediately above the room where the murdered man was to make sure the perp didn't get out the window and haul himself up to the second floor. And I checked the roof. Nothing. No disturbance of any kind. Forensic guy used luminol on the area immediately above the window just in case."

"Nothing?"

"Nothing."

"So he must have flown out."

Standbow thought that was funny. "Hardly likely. The perp was just a little cleverer than we are. But give us a bit of think time, and we'll figure it out. The perp and the body didn't just vanish."

"Anything else you can tell me about the room?"

"Only what I have heard. It was empty of any personal effects—and, of course, no body. Someone had been in the room, or at least messed it up for two nights. Other than that, goose egg."

"OK," Noonan said as he smiled. "That takes care of the forensics. As to the second part of your answer, what did you, that is, the Washakie Police Department do?"

"The usual, which, in the case of a small town like this, did not take long. We started searching for any car that might have been associated with the deceased. We did a circular search around the hotel, getting farther and farther from the scene of the crime. We ran about a hundred plates. Five came back from rental-car agencies, but we matched people to their rented car within the hour. Checked with the bus terminal. Of course, you've already talked to Sandy. Asked the state troopers to stop traffic on the highway, which they did. We got all the names and licenses of everyone from the roadblocks. All of them checked out, and no one fit the description of the deceased. We ran the road over Cannibal Pass and got nothing."

"Maybe the perp was long gone by the time the roadblock went up."

"Maybe. We don't have a time of death. The forensic people haven't given us a time yet. They are also running the DNA through the national database. But it is going to take six or eight weeks. We might get lucky."

"Not lucky for Mr. Harrison."

"If there was a Mr. Harrison."

This took Noonan by surprise. "You think there might not have been a murder?"

"I'm not sure of anything. But all the evidence points away from a murder. I mean, where's the body? Anyone can splash blood around a room and then change his—or her—bloody clothes. Heck, the victim himself could have done it. Go into his own room, splash a lot of blood around, strip off his bloody clothes, put on a jump suit, change shoes, put them into a garbage bag, and then walk out the door. If he did it after about ten p.m., there was only one person at the front desk. The victim could have carried the garbage bag out the back exit, and the person at the front desk would never have known he was gone. The Frank M. Canton Hotel doesn't have any security cameras, so it would have been easy."

"Then where'd the blood come from?"

"Blood bank, maybe. I don't know. Human blood is not hard to come by. You could buy it from derelicts for twenty dollars a pint or quart or whatever size is standard. Then splash it all over the room to make it look like a murder had taken place. Then skedaddle out of town. If the victim faked his own death at, say ten p.m., he could have been picked up by someone on the highway within fifteen minutes and been in Casper or Cheyenne before the sun came up. He would have beat the roadblocks by a dozen hours."

"Could he be hiding in town?"

Standbow shook his head and gave a kind of a shrug and smiled. "Very doubtful. Like I said before, we're a small town. Everyone knows everyone else's business. We didn't do a house-to-house, but we did check the empty buildings, hostels, high-school outbuildings, and the derelict shacks we know about. Nothing. If the victim had been hiding, we would have found him two days later when the Bodacious brothers got robbed. We did another thorough search for the perps in the robbery. And we had roadblocks up within minutes of that robbery. All we got from the roadblocks were names, addresses, and plate numbers. They all checked out."

"Did someone run the road through Cannibal Pass?"

"Yup. State Troopers had the exit onto the interstate closed within minutes. No one was on that road, and there was no indication anyone had used the road in days."

"So the perps in the Bodacious robbery just vanished."

"Seems so. We, that is, the Washakie Police Department, were shorthanded that day. Two of us had to take the other Mr. Harrison to Casper. Department strength was three officers for the three days Chief Standing Bear and I were in Cheyenne or traveling to and from."

"You and the chief weren't here when the Bodacious robbery took place?"

"Correct, but the other three in the department are no slouches. They left no stone unturned."

"And they found nothing."

"Nothing. And the perps were identifiable even at a distance. One, the man, was well over six feet tall, and the other, possibly a woman, was under five feet. There was nothing big happening in town like a rodeo or roundup, so they couldn't fade into a crowd."

"I hear that one of the Bodacious brothers has the robbery on tape."

Standbow laughed. "Tape? Naw. On a baby cam. Terrible picture, bad angle, no date and time stamp. You can see it if you want. The robbery was pretty quick. The two came in with masks, Elvis and Snow White, waved some guns around, grabbed some coins, and were out the door. You can't see it on the tape, but they ran about a block and then hit the jewelry store."

"You sure the robbery actually happened on that day?"

"I can't think of a reason for the Bodacious brothers to lie. They didn't get anything out of the robberies. Probably lost money. They didn't own the loot stolen. It was all consignment. Or almost all consignment. The insurance company paid up, but the Bodacious brothers didn't get much."

"You did a similar search for the perps? You searched for them just like you did Harrison?"

"Same pattern, yeah. Nothing."

"They just vanished."

"I don't like the way you said that."

"Sorry. But it's hard for me to believe that you can have two high-profile crimes in a town this size and have three people simply vanish."

"They did not *vanish*, to use your term. We just have not found them yet. Just like in a Las Vegas magician's act, people do not *vanish*."

"OK, moving on. What happened when the second Harrison showed up?"

"That was an interesting call. I got it. He was still haggling with the desk clerk when I got there. He wanted his key, and Harriett, the . . ."

"I've met her."

"Sharp lady, no nonsense. She stalled him until I got there."

"Did he seem surprised to see you arrive?"

Standbow was silent for a very long moment. "Mr. Harrison is a very odd duck. He is not a normal person. By that I do not mean he is a psychopath. I mean you cannot have a conversation with him. He is dislocated from reality. He's the kind of person you see walking down the street talking to himself or pushing a cart on a sidewalk full of whatever. I'd say he was a vet wandering the countryside. Homeless."

"What was he doing in Casper? He came to Washakie from Casper, right?"

"Casper. That's right. The address we had for him, that is, the alibi, was a homeless shelter. He was there for the evening meals and the nights. The rest of the time he was on the street."

"So that's what Chief Standing Bear meant when he said that alibi was not solid."

"That's right. After he showed up at the Frank M. Canton Hotel, we, that is Chief Standing Bear and I, took him to the psychiatric hospital in Casper. He didn't care. Like old-home week. I'm sure he's been in psychiatric hospitals before. My bet, our Mr. Harrison of day one gave Mr. Harrison of day three money and identification. Drove him to Washakie and pointed him in the direction of the Frank M. Canton Hotel. Said, 'There's a room for you there; just ask for the key.' Then Mr. Harrison of Day One who is not dead drove out of town. While Chief Standing Bear and I were questioning Mr. Harrison of Day Three, Mr. Harrison of Day One was putting miles between Washakie and his back bumper."

"Good call, but why?"

"I have no idea. I'm a cop, and I am used to simple crimes like murder, robbery, burglary, running a red light and DVs. Someone went to a lot of trouble to steer us up a very steep path that went nowhere with Mr. Harrison Day Three."

"And there is no money missing anywhere in town? No valuable that might have been stolen while you were distracted with the two Harrisons?"

"Nothing valuable. The museum has some antiques, which might be worth a few thousand, but nothing's missing. No one's robbed the bank or any of the gas stations. You know about the robbery of the Bodacious brothers two days after Mr. Harrison Day Three was taken to Casper. But no seems to have made a dime out of that robbery. No reason for the Bodacious brothers to stage a robbery where they get nothing out it."

"Are they the kind of people who might consider it?"

"They are cockroaches. Yeah, if they figure a way to scam the system for a buck or two. But they didn't get anything out the robbery. Just headaches."

CHAPTER 14

It had not been hard getting historically accurate paper. It had been very easy. All it took was a visit to an historical archive. Even easier was to find a book printed in the decade. Wyoming had scads of used bookstores and antique shops. Buy a book out of the 1860s and see if it had blank pages in the back. Take a razor blade, and zip; you then had a sheet of paper that would be authenticated to the 1860s.

Ink took a bit more research—but not that much more. Matching ink from 1670s would have been hard but not the 1870s. The real problem was the pen. The writing had to look authentic, and it would not be authentic it if were done with a fountain pen. It required a quill, and there were just not that many of them around. They had to be made.

There was a lot of money resting on the documents. They were going to be discovered as forgeries, but that was not the point. The point was the documents had to withstand scrutiny for about six months.

After that it didn't matter. Then it would be someone else's problem. Or the courts—and the courts never did anything fast. Five, ten years from now, someone would be squealing like a stuck pig. But it wouldn't be anyone in the cabal.

Time was on their side. The transfers would go through. Money would be exchanged. Everyone who wanted to get gone would go. Those who wanted to stay could stay, but it was on their heads if anything went wrong. But what could go wrong? There were going to be three arm's length transactions in a row. It would take the IRS and the SEC years to sort out the rat's nest of documents.

Right now it was just a matter of time.

The clock was ticking.

All they had to do was continue the misdirection.

So . . . catch me if you can!

CHAPTER 15

Police Officer Harold Standbow had been right on when it came to the character of the Bodacious brothers: they were human cockroaches. Everything about them pulsed cheap, sleazy, and untrustworthy. Why anyone would consign coins or jewelry to them was beyond Noonan.

Until he found out that there was only one coin store in Washakie. It was owned by Harry Bodacious. Sam Bodacious had the only jewelry story in town—if you didn't count the jewelry aisle in the Washakie grocery store. If you had gems to sell, you had to deal with Sam Bodacious. For coins, it was Harry.

The baby-cam recording was as cheap as the brothers were. Yes, it did show a robbery, but the picture was grainy, old, and gave no indication of date much less the time of day. It showed nothing clearly, just a robbery that was at most two minutes in length. Two perpetrators, one about two inches over six feet in an Elvis mask with a gun holding up the coin store. The other perpetrator, who walked like a woman, scooped up the coins. Then the pair headed for the door. Harry could be seen heading for the phone as the perpetrators left the store.

Noonan tried to find at least one nice thing to say about the baby-cam tape.

He couldn't.

So he didn't try.

"This is the worst security tape I have ever seen."

"Well," said Harry Bodacious flippantly, "we never expected to be robbed, so we didn't spend a lot of money on security equipment."

"Do tell," snipped Noonan. "At the very least you could have bought a new baby cam."

"Why?" asked Harry. "Why spend the money on something we didn't think we'd need? I got the baby cam used. Salvation Army store. Then I put sign in the front window saying we had surveillance cameras."

"Apparently, that did the trick," Noonan said flatly.

"Works in the movies," Harry responded defensively. "And the sign cost more than the baby cam."

"For good reason," Noonan was purposely flippant. "This tape is worthless."

"Not so," cut in Sam Bodacious. "It shows the two robbers. One is a tall man and the other, a short one. Probably a woman. Even I can tell that by the way she walks and stands."

Noonan looked over his shoulder and gave Sam a sarcastic look that read *Really!*

"What's the problem here?" Harry cut in. "You're not here to investigate the robbery. That's Leonard's job, Chief Standing Bear. You shouldn't even be here."

"I go where crime is," Noonan said softly. "This is a crime close in time to the supposed murder of person unknown in your small town. There is a chance this crime is related."

"Related to what?" wailed Sam. "The dead guy wasn't a six-foot-two man or a woman under five feet! The robbery happened days after the dead guy was, well, dead. We know these two robbers ain't the dead man 'cause we've got 'em on tape, and they ain't the other Harrison guy because he's in the loony bin in Casper."

"I don't know there isn't a connection," Noonan said quietly. "When I am sure there isn't a connection, I'll stop asking questions."

71

"But there isn't a connection!" Harry said with exasperation. "We didn't make a dime on the robbery! The robbers got the coins and gems"—he pointed at Sam—"and we didn't own the coins or the gems. The insurance company paid us, and we had to pay the people who actually owned the coins and gems."

"True," said Noonan. "But the coins and gems are still in the wind. That's thousands unaccounted for."

"Ppppllleeeaaasseee." Sam dragged out the word. "First, if we had stolen the *coins and gems*," he accented the words *coins and gems* as if it were a slur, "we'd still have to sell them. By law we have to check the gems. So we do. We've got them on Gemprint. Do you know what that is?"

Noonan nodded as he was writing in his notebook. He didn't say anything, so Sam went on.

"So if we had stolen the gems and tried to sell them, the gem fingerprint would pop up as stolen. Then we'd go to jail. For a whole of what six thousand dollars? That was the value of the gems stolen."

Harry added, "The coins, yes, they could be sold because they do not have a provenance. But that's only six thousand dollars. I spend that much keeping my store open for a month, month and a half. It doesn't make much sense to risk ten years in jail for six thousand dollars."

"I never said you two robbed your own stores," Noonan tried to add.

"You sure insinuated it," Sam said stumbling over the word *insinuated*. "We're just a couple of honest businessmen trying to make a living."

"Good for you," Noonan added. "America needs businessmen like you two. Just a couple of more questions. When did you call the police?" Noonan looked at Sam.

"He didn't call the police; I did," cut in Harry.

"Well, when the police were called, how long before they arrived?"

"Minutes," replied Harry.

"Then they went from the coin store to the jewelry story. Is that right?"

"The cops or the robbers?"

"Both."

"Correct. The robbers started in the coin store and went to the jewelry store. The cops came to the coin store, and while they were here, they got the call that the jewelry store had been robbed."

"So the cops went to the jewelry store?"

"No," said Harry. "We have a police force of six in town. One was on vacation and two—Chief Standing Bear and Harold Standbow—were in Casper with the loony. Two cops were here in the coin store, and the third cop, Johnny whateverhisnameis, went to the jewelry store. Then they hooked up and put out the call to the state troopers to close off the highway."

"How long did that take?"

"Ten minutes, maybe."

"So the thieves had ten minutes to get out of town."

"Sounds about right."

"Apparently, they made it."

"Well," said Sam cautiously, "they weren't stopped at the roadblocks, and they're not in town, so that doesn't leave much."

"True, true," Noonan added. "Just a couple of more things. Did the thieves take anything other than the coins and gems?"

"Like what?" asked Harry.

"Well," Noonan said looking around, "the two of your shops sell more than just coins and gems. Did they take anything other than coins and gems?"

"Nothing else of value in the stores," Sam said. "No, not from my shop."

"Or from mine," added Harry.

"How about footprints and fingerprints. Did the police find any?"

Sam laughed. "The robbers were wearing gloves, so no to fingerprints. Footprints? Be serious! This is Wyoming in August. Every square foot of every shop in town is covered with dust and footprints. Did the robbers leave footprints? Sure. Can you distinguish them from every other footprint on the floor? Unlikely."

"Any other questions," snipped Harry.

"Just one. How many consignments did you have all together?"

"Coins, a lot," said Harry, speaking for the brothers. "Coins are small-ticket items. Jewels, three. They are big-ticket items. Two of them were inheritance sales, a brother and sister in Des Moines. They've never been here. Their uncle died in town. They sold his house, donated his furniture to the Episcopal church, and consigned his gem collection. The third was Joshua Three Trees. He's a Native. We don't know where he got his gems, but they passed the Gemprint test, so they're legal."

"Is he part of the Nimerigar group?"

"Every Native in this neck of the woods is in Nimerigar—and we don't have any woods here."

CHAPTER 16

Mr. Harrison Day Three was having a great day.

It had started with breakfast.

Not just breakfast but BREAKFAST!

The slop he had been eating in the homeless shelters was swill compared to this meal. Well, that was the price of being homeless. Even if it was for a week. Here in the facility the food was pretty good. Roommates, not so much. There was a real reason they were in here. Very good reasons. That was fine with him. He wasn't going to be here very long. He only had one task: delay. Delay whoever showed up. That wouldn't be hard. He'd been fooling juries for two decades. This was going to be his *pièce de résistance*.

And his swan song.

CHAPTER 17

Johnny Whateverhisnameis was actually Jon Strano. He looked Filipino but was six one. He had baby-blond hair but jet-black eyes. His uniform fit as though it had been tailored for him, but his clodhoppers gave him the appearance of a sodbuster in the city who bought a pair of shoes to fit in with the crowd. But the minute he opened his mouth it was clear this man was no country hick.

Noonan caught up with him at the Washakie Café. The moment Noonan walked into the diner, Strano waved him over.

"I hear you're looking for me," he said with a smile.

"If you're Jon Strano."

"Come on, Captain. Everyone in town knows who you are even if they've never laid eyes on you. Asking all kinds of questions. And"—his right hand swept the packed diner—"I know everyone here. So you have to be Captain Heinz Noonan of the Sandersonville Police Department. And"—he leaned forward confidentially as his left hand pulled the chair alongside the table out so Noonan could sit down—"you're not wearing boots. You and I are the only two people in town who don't wear boots."

Noonan chuckled and shook his head as he sat down. "I know why I don't wear cowboy boots. Why don't you?"

"Too hard to run in them. I'm not theater. When I have to move, I want to move fast. Cowboy boots are for show these days. Pinched toes and heels high enough for spurs. Now, what can I do for you? I don't know anything you haven't been told before."

"Well," Noonan said as he sat down, "you never know. Can I get a cup of coffee before we talk?"

Strano indicated the counter with his left hand. "It's on me." With his right hand, he attracted the attention of the cashier and made a motion saying, 'I'm paying for him.' The clerk smiled, and when Noonan came to pay, the clerk shook her head and jerked it in Strano's direction.

"Mighty kind of you," Noonan said as he sat down.

"We're mighty friendly here in the Badlands," he said. "We don't get that many illustrious visitors here. Cowboys, yes. Ranchers, yes. Buckle bunnies and historians are a dime a dozen. The closest we have to crime fighters are the four teenage mutant Ninja turtles."

"They make it this far west?"

"Yes, sir. Every Saturday morning."

"I just had a few questions."

"You professionals always do. You don't look like Columbo."

"I dress better, but I'd like to think I'm just as smart." Noonan pulled out his notebook and flipped through some pages.

"Word on the street is that you are. Let me make your job easy. When the call came in regarding Mr. Harrison on day three, I never made the Frank M. Canton Hotel. I was ordered to cover the road over Cannibal Pass. I drove all the way over the pass to the interstate and sat with a Wyoming State Trooper for three hours to make sure no one tried to slip out of town."

"Did anyone?"

"Slip out of town? There were three or four carloads. We checked everyone's ID, recorded the names. Yes. There was no one I didn't know at least casually. Like I said, we're a small town."

"Actually, I'm more interested in the robberies."

"I was told you'd ask that. I was at the bus terminal when the call came in about the robbery. I went directly to the Bodacious jewelry store and basically guarded Sam until the other two officers got there. I spent the next three, four hours doing inventory with Sam Bodacious and matched up missing jewelry boxes with consignment sheets."

"So you never saw the robbers?"

"That's correct. We, that is, the three officers on duty, did a Q&D." He paused for a moment. "Do you know what a Q&D is?"

"Quick and Dirty," Noonan replied. "When you have to do something important but don't have the time to do it meticulously."

"Right. We did a Q&D of vehicles in town. The state troopers had a roadblock up in a matter of minutes. They checked IDs and car trunks and searched vans and every Winnebago for the next twelve hours. They came up empty. No one matching the description came through the roadblocks."

"You searched in town as well?"

"Not every door but, yeah, in town as well. You can't hide in this town."

"Nothing?"

"*Niento*. Or, as you say in English . . ."

"Nothing," Noonan replied. "I speak a little Italian."

Noonan was looking at his notes when Strano asked if he wanted more coffee. Noonan nodded yes. Strano got up and asked if he wanted cream and sugar. Noonan just said "black" and pointed to a pile of cream capsules on the table. When Strano got back to the table, Noonan had found the spot in his journal he needed.

"You said that you got the call to go to the Bodacious jewelry store while you were at the bus terminal. Something about an alarm. Was there a fire at the bus terminal that day?"

"It was a false alarm. A tour bus had stopped for diesel when it started smoking. The smoke was pretty thick, and it set off the fire alarm. I came over from police headquarters and checked out the situation."

"No one injured?"

"No. Just a lot of smoke."

"What color was the smoke?"

This took Strano by surprise. "What color was the smoke? Smoke is, well, smoke."

"Not really. It's not as if there are lots of kinds of smoke. Generally speaking, there are three kinds of smoke: dark or black, white, and blue. Do you remember what color the smoke was?"

"No. Not really. Why not ask the terminal manager? I wasn't there very long before I got the call to go to the Bodacious jewelry store."

"Was anyone else at the terminal when the bus started to smoke?"

"Well, yeah. Every volunteer firefighter in town. Like everyone tells you, we're a small town. When there's a fire, we respond."

"How many firefighters do you have in Washakie?"

"I can't give you an actual number. I think there are six firepeople—two are women—who are sort of full time. I say *sort of* because everyone here has more than one job."

"Do you have more than on job?"

"I lied. A lot of people have more than one job. I'm not sure about the firepeople and if they have other jobs. But the city pays for six. Then there are another six or seven volunteers."

"Did the volunteers show up at the fire?"

Strano gave Noonan a look that read "Really?"

Noonan got the message. "So all of the volunteers came?"

"I saw four or five. Then I got the call, so I left. I left Brenda Maple in charge. To do the paperwork, I mean. She's pretty competent. She works for the county in the county building."

"Did she file a report?"

"Got it right here," Strano said as he pawed through a pile of papers Noonan could not see on the seat of a chair beside him. "I knew you were coming, so I made a copy." Strano handed him two sheets of paper. "Brenda is quite competent. I have no idea why you want this, but here's a copy."

"How did you know I'd be asking for this?" Noonan asked as he jiggled the paper.

"I'm psychic," said Strano with a smile. "Everyone said you were thorough." Then he leaned forward, "And it's the only paperwork I have that has anything to do with the Harrisons or Bodacious brothers."

"You are good at your jobs, sir. Is there anything you can tell me—since you are psychic—that I don't know that will help me?"

"Nothing that would stand up in court."

"I'm all ears."

"I'd say the Harrison murder and the robberies are connected. How I do not know."

"Why do you say that?"

"This is a small town. We know everything about everyone in town."

"I've heard that before," Noonan said smiling. "Everyone keeps telling me."

"I can imagine," Strano replied. "But two odd events happening so close to one another in a town where nothing ever happens, well, there has got to be a connection."

"You may be right," Noonan looked at his notes. "Just one more thing."

"You sure you are not channeling Columbo?"

"I'm not psychic, remember. You are."

"Got me there."

"The bus that was smoking. It was fixed there in the terminal?"

"Don't know. But it was running fine an hour or two later. It came through the roadblock on the highway."

"You searched the bus?"

"Top, bottom, storage space, and I even crawled under the bus to make sure no one was up inside any hollow under the bus."

"No suspects."

"Not the guy. He was well over six feet. The tour bus was all women, and a few of them were about five feet tall. We ran their IDs and got matches. I've got their names if you need them."

"Bus driver not over six feet?"

"Short, squat. Over six feet around, not tall."

CHAPTER 18

Cell phones were a gift of the gods. They made Philadelphia, Nassau, Georgetown, and Washakie as close as neighbors in a subdivision. Closer, actually. This was particularly true when it came to money. Banking was at the speed of light. Even more important, news of banking—specifically, transactions—were a click away. Then, when all was said and done, the phones could go ghost. Be gone. Deep in the blue sea, roasting in the Badlands, or buried in a landfill. The clock was ticking.

CHAPTER 19

Joshua Three Trees was exactly what his name described—except that the three trees were one on top of the other. Three Trees was the tallest man Noonan had ever seen. But then again, Noonan was not a basketball fan. Three Trees might have been seven feet tall. Noonan didn't know, but he did have to look up to talk to him.

It did not take Noonan long to realize that he was in way over his head.

One sentence.

"I have nothing to say to the occupying forces."

"Sorry?"

"Occupying forces. You whites. Take our land. Steal our women. Leave us in the wilderness with nothing to starve and die."

"That's quite a charge."

"Do you have a warrant?"

"I'm not here to arrest you. I'm here to talk about your jewelry consignment at the Bodacious . . ."

Before he could complete the sentence, the front door slammed in his face.

CHAPTER 20

"He has come and gone."
"What did he ask?"
"Consignment only."
"Nothing else?"
"Never had a chance to ask."
"Keep it that way."
"No other way to have it."

CHAPTER 21

"Nelvis Thompson and don't ask."

"I can imagine what it is most people ask." Noonan gave a sly smile as he shook the Wyoming state trooper's hand in the hole-in-the-wall trooper substation in the back of what would have been called mall in North Carolina but was advertised as the Washakie Shopping Center. Thompson offered Noonan a chair in front of the paper-littered desk as he spoke.

"Thanks for not asking."

"I'm discrete. I'm . . ."

"Oh, I know who you are. Everyone in town does.

"Let me guess; it's a small town and . . ."

"Everybody's told you, so I don't have to. And you want to called Heinz, right?"

"As rain."

"Since I had nothing to do with the murder investigation or the robberies but ran the blockade, I'll take a wild guess and suggest that's why you're here."

"Everyone in this town is psychic."

Thompson laughed. "No. We're a small town and, well, you know the rest." He scrounged around on the piles of paper on his desk and came up

84

with six sheets of paper, all of them in sets of two and stapled. He handed Noonan one set of sheets. "This is the list of everyone stopped going either direction after the Harrison murder." Then he handed Noonan another set of stapled sheets. "And this is the list of everyone stopped going either direction after the Bodacious robberies." He handed Noonan the final set of stapled sheets. "Finally, assuming you were going to ask for it, these are all the people stopped on the Cannibal Pass road after the murder and robberies. And before you ask, yes, we compared all lists and came up with no duplicates."

"You are to be commended for you work."

"Just because we live in Wyoming doesn't mean we do slipshod work."

Noonan took the lists, folded them, wrote on them, and slipped them into his notebook. Indicating the lists by tapping on their folded edges he said, "About how many of these people do you know or are local?"

"Almost all of them. The only exception was the busload of tourists. All women and I didn't know any of them."

"Are their names listed here?"

"Only the ones who were under about five two." That was the description of the woman in the Bodacious robbery."

"How many women were on the bus?"

"Oh, I don't know. More than fifteen and less than thirty. City folks on some kind of bird-watching expedition."

"They were on the bus that was smoking?"

"It wasn't smoking when we stopped it."

Noonan was silence for a moment. Then he asked, "Was the bus in Washakie being repaired when the Bodacious robberies went down?"

"Had to be. Otherwise we would not have stopped the bus."

"Did the bus start smoking before the robberies?"

"Again. Had to be. I think I, we, the troopers, were told the women had about an hour or so in town while the smoking problem was solved. That would be about the time of the robberies. But"—and he raised his hand to stop a question by Noonan—"there was absolutely, positively, no woman on that bus who was under five two" that is not on the list in your hand. The bus driver was a lot shorter than the six feet whatever, and the Washakie cop, Johnny Strano, went over that bus with a fine-tooth comb. Checked the luggage compartment and under the engine hood. Even crawled the length of the bus on his back to make sure no one was hiding in some hollow over the drive shaft."

"Could any of the other vehicles have had hidden compartments?"

"Nope. Like I said, even though we're in Wyoming, we don't do slipshod work."

"Well, then, since you are from Wyoming. If a man six feet two and a woman under five feet robbed a pair of Washakie stores in broad daylight and they can't be found in town and aren't picked up at a roadblock, where are they?"

"If I knew that"—he smiled humorously—"I'd be the chief of detectives in some town on the North Carolina beach."

CHAPTER 22

The stack of papers was not very heavy. But then again, it didn't have to be heavy to be worth $20 million. It was going to be a three-way transfer, so no one was going to be left holding the bag. But it was going to be tricky.

Had this been a straight transfer, a simple sale, the papers would have gone from seller to buyer with no intermediary. But that was not the way the deal had to go down. It was seller to an intermediary who would transfer ownership to a third party. At the same time, the third party was paying, the intermediary was buying a pig in a poke. But that pig was a multimillion-dollar pig, and for $20 million, it was worth the risk. Even then, the paperwork had to be so buried and dispersed that it would take an army of auditors to ferret out the responsibles.

But not the blame.

That was the joy of being too big to prosecute. If worse came to worst, it would all be handled sub rosa. Even if not, in this business there was no such thing as bad publicity. Most delicious of all, money paid for penalties had one of two specific legally insulating caveats: *tax deductions* and *cost of doing business*.

She would be the only person on the dodge. She didn't care. Where she was going, she would not even have to file with the IRS. Her partners could file with the IRS. They had done nothing illegal. Business was business.

There was only one more shoe to fall.

CHAPTER 23

"Blue." The bus-station manager, ticket agent, and janitor had no trouble at all remembering the tour-bus smoke.

"You sure?"

"Been in the business about as long as you've been a cop. Blue."

"Do you have this problem often—bus smoking?"

"Yeah. Not all the time. Upon occasion. Let me put it another way. It's not unusual."

"Anything unusual about this occasion?"

"Not that I can think of. Bus pulled in and started to smoke, alarm went off, and we cleared the terminal."

"Why did you clear the terminal? Is a smoking bus dangerous?"

"No, but my insurance agent is. Any hint of danger to a person, we have to evacuate the terminal."

"Do you do this every time a bus smokes?"

"Only if the alarm goes off. Then my insurance agent knows there's a problem. She's a volunteer with the Washakie Fire Department. When she shows up, I clear the terminal."

"In the last month, how many smoking buses have come into the terminal?"

"All of them. Buses smoke all the time. You just don't see it when the bus is moving. When the bus comes into the terminal, the exhaust starts to fill the room. The bus turns the engine off, no more exhaust."

"Was the tour bus smoking when it came into the terminal?"

"Must have been."

"But you're not sure."

"That's right. The tour bus came in. Smoke started to fill the terminal. The smoke alarm went off. I cleared the terminal because I knew my insurance agent was going to be coming to the 'scene of the fire.'"

"Are you sure the smoke set off the alarm?"

"Pretty sure. Why?"

"Just wondering. Is there a way to find out?"

"Sure. It takes a day or two. But yeah, why?"

"Because I'm a curious kind of guy."

The bus-station manager, ticket agent, and janitor laughed. "Sure. Whatever. But even if I find someone set of the alarm, so what? The terminal was filling with smoke. There were people coming off the bus, probably some still inside the bus. It would have been a good idea to hit an alarm."

"If they knew where to find them."

"State of Wyoming makes sure *you can* find them. Any more questions?"

"One more. What day do you take out the garbage?"

"From the terminal?"

"Yes."

"Inside or outside?"

"Is there a difference?"

"There are two kinds of inside garbage. One is what you would call *trash*. That's plastic pop bottles, facial tissue, food wrappers, paper cups. When the garbage can fills up, we wrap up the plastic liner and set it out back. The second kind of inside trash is from the mechanical end of the business: oily rags, empty oil cans, broken bolts, stuff like that. Which trash are you talking about?"

"Both."

"OK. The filled plastic bags go out Thursday morning. The trash company picks up the bags early in the morning. The other trash we take to a special landfill. We are environmentally conscious here in the Badlands." The second sentence was said with sarcasm.

"So the plastic bag from the day of the alarm is gone."

"Four, five days gone."

"Thanks."

"How about the smoke? Don't you want to know what happened to the smoke?"

This took Noonan by surprise. "The smoke? Where did it go?"

"The Great Smoky Mountains. Where do you think the mountain range gets its smoke?" Then the bus-station manager, ticket agent, and janitor laughed. "Just a joke. I'll see what I can find about the alarm, but I don't know what help it will do you."

CHAPTER 24

Harrison Day Three was pleased to meet with his lawyer. Or, as they say in Wyoming, *loyer*. His *loyer* was a public defender from the State of Wyoming who told him the same thing that day as on the first: keep your mouth shut. That was fine with Harrison Day Three.

He didn't have anything to say.

Actually, this was not true. He had been doing quite a bit of talking. To himself. In public, so to speak, in the psychiatric-holding facility. This was part of the plan. He only had to do four things publicly, in order, all of them legal:

1. Show up at the Frank M. Canton Hotel and claim to be someone he was not.
2. Allow himself to be taken to Casper for a psychiatric hold.
3. Talk to some cop from North Carolina.
4. Vanish.

He didn't know when the cop from North Carolina was going to come. But his *loyer* would tell him. The conversation would be his final act. Then he'd be in the wind.

CHAPTER 25

Oddly, and for Heinz Noonan, the "Bearded Holmes," who got the heebie-jeebies if he was too far from ocean salt water, he had always wanted to visit Casper, Wyoming. It wasn't something on his bucket list in the sense that he wouldn't have missed some great life adventure by not going. Rather, it was because he wanted to walk along the Platte River.

Why?

Because, like the coast of North Carolina, it had a ghostship. The environs of Sandersonville included the stretch of ocean where the *Carrol A. Deering* was discovered. The *Carrol A. Deering* had been a schooner with five masts which had run aground off Cape Hatteras in 1921, just up the coast from Sandersonville. Unlike other ships that had run aground, this one had no crew. All navigation equipment was gone as was the ship's log—along with two lifeboats and all the crew's personal property including clothing and seabags. And, most perplexing, food for a meal was being prepared when whatever happened. After an exhaustive investigation by the US Departments of the Treasury, Justice, the Navy, State, Revenue, and the US Coast Guard, no definitive answer was ever found. Half a century later the fate of the *Carrol A. Deering* was attributed to the mysterious forces of the Bermuda Triangle.

What fascinated Noonan was a similar tale of the Platte River. In this case, it was the Death Ship or Phantom Ship of the Platte.

The ship did not have a name.

It just appeared.

If that was all, then it would have been nothing more than grist in the ongoing maybe-strange-but-true tales of the Badlands—stories like the Big Nose George's skin shoes, the jackalope, and the Pedro Mountain Mummy. Supposedly, the Death Ship of the Platte River first appeared in 1862 when a trapper by the name of Leon Webber alleged that he saw a phantom ship—its sails and mast coated with ice—preceding a massive fogbank, moving up the Platte River. History does not record if Webber had been drinking at the time, but it is hard to believe a man in the Badlands in those years would not have had a few at any time of day. There were also no witnesses to this sighting, it should be added. Supposedly, again, according to Webber, a frozen crew was on deck who, according to Wikipedia, were "huddled around a corpse on a canvas sheet." This was a portending of a person's doom, which, in the case of Webber—again according to Wikipedia—was Webber's fiancé who "died later that same day." It is unclear how Webber, clearheaded or not, from shore, could have seen a corpse of anyone lying on a sheet of canvas on the deck of a ship in motion—and a many-masted schooner at that—in the middle of a river. Where Webber's fiancé was at the time is unclear.

Unclear also was the location of Gene Wilson's wife on that tragic day in 1886 when Wilson reported seeing the same ship. Again, he was onshore, Wilson swore he had seen the "body of his wife laid out on the canvas." Yet again, in 1903, one Victor Heibe was chopping down a tree on the banks of the Platte River when he saw the ship, and, again, on the canvas was "the body of a close friend who died the same day."

It was never discovered why the ship was only seen in late fall. Then there was the question of why a multimasted schooner would be in a river named *Plat* by the French, which translated to *Flat* in English. Pioneers knew the river as the *Plat*, and more than one described it as "a mile wide and an inch deep." Further, the weather in Wyoming in the "late fall" was hardly conducive to an ice-laden multimasted schooner.

So, for Heinz Noonan to be headed up Highway 25 to Casper about the same time of the year as the appearance of the alleged Death Ship of the Platte River was a labor of historical love. After he had made his official rounds in Casper, he intended to drive the 111 miles to Guernsey and then go 6 miles southeast of town. Just in case, he kept telling himself, just in case, you know, the Death Ship of the Platte River made an appearance. He was not particularly interested in seeing anyone laid on a sheet of canvas, whether he knew them or not.

But then again there were some people . . .

Casper was the second-largest city in Wyoming, but even then it had barely sixty thousand people. That was miniscule by North Carolina standards. Nevertheless, the city reeked of the history of the West. In this case, *West* was a part of the country, not a direction. The city had been established on the site of Fort Casper, which had been built in the middle of the eighteen hundreds because it had been an ideal location for ferries to cross—of course, the Platte River. Not only did the military protect the river crossing but the telegraph and mail service too, which followed. The name *Casper* came from the son of Colonel Collins, the namesake of Fort Collins. True to the tradition of Wyoming oddly, Fort Collins, the city, was named after a fort that was never built there. Caspar Collins had been killed by Indians in the area. The garrison then known as the Platte Bridge Station was renamed *Caspar* in his honor. This fort had walls. Again, true to the tradition of Wyoming oddly, the cartographers misspelled *Caspar* as *Casper*, and the city's name remains *Casper* to the present day.

Troops were only in Fort Casper for about three months. It was abandoned in 1867 when the troops moved south and established Fort Fetterman, which was the site of the largest Indian massacre to date. On December 21, 1866, ten years before the Little Big Horn, Colonel William J. Fetterman and eighty soldiers were suckered into battle against Red Cloud and Crazy Horse. It was estimated that the eighty soldiers and Fetterman faced a horde of two thousand Indians who unleashed a rain of forty thousand arrows.

Chloe Fetterman, the State of Wyoming forensic specialist, made it clear she was related to William J. "Direct descendant of William's brother. You might say my roots are right here in Wyoming."

"And in the right city," commented Noonan. "It's good to know someone appreciates local history."

"No such thing as local history," she retorted. "It's all part of national history. What happens here affects everywhere, and what happens everywhere affects here. Chaos theory in action."

"I like your attitude," Noonan said as he sat down. "History is not the story of the past; it's the study of the future."

Fetterman—Chloe, not William J.—smiled. (Though it might have been possible for William J. to be smiling—in another dimension.) "With a name like Fetterman, in this state, at this time, you draw attention."

"You talking about the Nimerigar?"

"Today, yes. In the past, their predecessors. You're from North Carolina, so the population has become used to everyone living unhappily side by side. This is the West. The Sand Creek Massacre was last week. John Chivington was scum of the earth. It just so happened that he was white. There are plenty of cases of Indian Chivingtons. It's just not PC to bring them up."

"Ah, the stench of politics."

"Ah, yes. And now to business, what do you want to know?"

"And you know who I am?"

"We're a small state. No one ever comes to visit me. Yeah, you're either Captain Heinz Noonan of the Sandersonville, North Carolina, Police Department—who likes to be called Heinz—or the tooth fairy. I've got almost all of my adult teeth, so I'm betting you're Heinz."

"I give up. Whacha got?"

"Zip."

"You're the forensic guru for Wyoming, and you've got zip!"

"Politics, Heinz, politics. We have a state crime lab in Cheyenne. It wants to handle the big cases. Murder is a big case. So . . . we little people gather the evidence and send it to them. They do the actual forensics."

"Ah, the people of sweat and the people of show. The people of sweat do the work; the people of show take the credit."

"Same the whole world over. So what I've got is zip."

"Well, then tell what you can."

"I collected a lot of red blood. It was human blood. We did a field test. I'd say the blood was ten to twelve hours old when I collected it."

95

"How much was there?"

"Lots."

"So whoever it was could not be alive?"

"That's what I'd guess."

"I was told there was blood splatter."

"Careful with that term. It will take an expert to determine the details, and the expert we have . . ."

Noonan finished the sentence, ". . . is at the crime lab in Cheyenne and was not at the scene of the crime."

"Correct. So—for the moment—was there splatter? Yes. What kind of splatter, I don't know. I'm not an expert. But then again, there are enough forensic programs on television to clue anyone into making blood splatter. All you have to do is sling some bloody clothing around. There was blood splatter on the ceiling of the room, but that would be easy to fake."

"Footprints?"

"Easy to fake. Everything in that room screamed fake."

"Why so?"

"No body. No blood trail out of the room. No blood in the bathtub. No drag marks down the hallway. No personal effects in the room. No fingerprints. I'd say it was faked."

"Why?"

"Uh, uh, uh." She smiled and shook an index finger at him. "I'm the forensic person. You're the detective. I should be asking you that question."

"I don't want to break your heart, but I do not have the slightest idea. I'm used to finding the money angle and tracing it to the perpetrators."

"Well, I can't help you there. Officially, the room had lots of a red substance looking like blood. It smelled like blood. It was sticky like blood. I took samples, which I sent to the state crime lab for analysis and DNA testing. Good luck on getting results anytime soon. There were footprints in the red substance. There were no fingerprints. That's all I can say."

"It's enough. You have time for some wild questions?"

"I always have time for fantasies." She smiled.

"OK. Where's the money here?"

"I don't see a dime anywhere. The room was empty when I got there. The guy they took to the psychiatric facility here in town had no money in his wallet. No big bucks there."

"The Bodacious robberies in Washakie got the thieves all of about thirteen thousand dollars, which is p-r-e-t-t-y thin." Noonan shook his head. "I'll be visiting with the chiefs of police in Bridger and Colter. Anything I should know?"

"The cubed root of seventeen. No. This is Wyoming. Are those robberies related? Sure. Why not? Same MO and same suspects. Did the thieves get much? Nope. The only thing odd about the three is that the perps seemed to have disappeared after the crime. At least twice anyway. In Bridger and Washakie. Odd, you know. In towns that small to vanish. Bridger, well, that's another story. Fourth of July weekend and the rodeo was in town. Lots of six-foot-tall men with short women all over town. Dump the masks, and the perps would fit right in. Colter and Washakie, not so much."

"The Bridger robbery, then. Anything else odd?"

"Everything about Bridger is odd. It's a unique Wyoming town. It's historically odd because it has water—a lot of it. Even more important, it has a lake with easy access from the interstate. I don't know what you know about Wyoming, but water is a very big deal here—at least during the summer. If you've got water, you've got gold. Quite literally. Bridger is on a huge lake—Buckle Bunny Lake. Because it has the lake, it has a tourist industry. You can rent boats in Bridger and fish."

"Could the perps have taken a boat and sailed away?"

"Not in a sailboat. Powerboat, maybe, but I doubt it. State troopers have a chopper, and any boat on the water would be met with law enforcement. I haven't heard that any boat actually made it across the lake that day. It's a huge lake. All the boats rented that day came out of Bridger and came back that evening. The Bridger police are very good. They checked everyone out."

"Another case of vanishing then."

"Could be. But I doubt it. We just haven't figured out how they did it yet. Sorry I could not help you with the blood work. You'll have to wait a while for the DNA report. The state crime lab has it on low profile.

No body, no crime. There are other murders with bodies that have to be considered first."

"This is one time I agree with politics."

"Anything else I can help you with?"

Noonan thought for a moment. "Yeah, as a matter of fact. Do you have any kind of a mechanical person here? You know, someone who does forensics on vehicles."

"Not really. When the state crime lab doesn't take our case, we have someone who goes over a vehicle looking for blood, fingerprints, fiber. The usual. But you mean someone who knows engines. The best person to talk to Nels Birkenbinder. He manages the bus station here in Casper. Worked his way up from mechanic. A bit quirky. Thinks he's a reincarnated Viking. But he does know engines. When we have problems here, he does the repairs."

"Anything else I should know?"

"If you spend time out of a city, remember the explorer's code."

"Explorer's code?"

"Take nothing but photos. Leave nothing but footprints. Break nothing but silence. Kill nothing but time."

"Got it."

CHAPTER 26

Trust is a wonderful thing. It is also very fragile. Once broken, it is gone forever. He didn't care. He'd spent a lifetime building trust across the state. And it had got him nothing. It was not as if he was respected for it. He wasn't. He had just been another bureaucrat—usually said with a sneer. He had been the minion of the state. For a lifetime he had been the pebble in the shoe of corporations who were making more during his lunchbreak than he would make in a lifetime.

No more.

He was on a different wavelength now. He was in the right place at the right time. Even more important, he *knew* he was in the right place at the right time. Success, he was discovering, was more than sitting around and waiting for it to call. It was seizing the moment. Carpe diem.

Carpe diem was a fine quote to use in an English class, but it took more than that in real life. It meant taking a chance, marshaling your resources. Then you had to strike. You had to make your move. He would. He could. He had the keys to every county office in the state. Had had them for years. Now he was going to use them.

CHAPTER 27

When Chloe Fetterman had said that Nels Birkenbinder was a quirky Viking, Noonan had not been sure what she meant. But the moment he stepped into the Casper bus terminal, he knew exactly what she meant. Adorning the back wall of the terminal was a massive ceramic map of Norway with the mountain ranges supersized. Also supersized was a print of two men, clearly Norwegian, on skis whisking through a forest. Both men were only using one ski pole, and one of the men had what appeared to be a baby on his back.

As Noonan was taking a closer look at the print, Nels Birkenbinder came out of his office at the back of the terminal. If Hollywood studios were ever to be looking for the perfect Viking, Birkenbinder was their man. As tall as Noonan, he had a full head of long red hair and beard to match. If there was an ounce of fat on him, it was well hidden. Broad at the shoulders and narrow at the hips, his jumpsuit fit him perfectly. Had he been at the prow of a Viking vessel with horns on the steerer's head, he would have been a perfect fit—except for the jumpsuit.

"Thorstein Skevla and Skjervald Skrukka," he said proudly as he pointed at the print. "Do you know the story?"

"Actually, no. Is that a baby on the back of one of them?"

"Not just a *baby*, the future and greatest king of Norway. Haakon Haakonsson. For more than a century, there had been open civil war between the Birkenbeiners and Baglers."

"Birkenbeiners. Like your name?"

"Absolutely. Birkenbeiners. Named because when they were poor, they wore trousers made of birchbark. In 1203, the Birkenbeiner king was poisoned and a new king elected. What no one knew at the time was that the king had a son, an infant at the time. That was the good news. The bad news was that the child, eighteen months old, was living the territory of the Birkenbeiners' mortal foe, the Baglers. So a band of Birkenbeiners slipped into Bagler territory and took the child."

"Let me guess," said Noonan pointing to the print. "The Baglers found out about the child and sent their assassins."

"Because of a *traitor!*" Bierkenbeiner said with venom in his voice. "To make sure child lived, a collection of Bierkenbeiners held up the Baglers while the two greatest skiers in the history of Norway"—he pointed to the print—"Thorstein Skevla and Skjervald Skrukka spirited the baby hundreds of miles to Nidaors. They all survived, and the child ushered in the Norwegian Golden Age."

"I'm impressed," said Noonan. "Just don't ask me to repeat any of those names."

Bierkenbeiner laughed. "It's not easy being a Viking in Wyoming. But you're not here to talk about Vikings. You want to know about buses."

"How did you know that?"

"Wyoming is a very small town with a very long street. What can I do for you?"

"Tell me about smoke from a bus."

"All buses smoke just like all cars smoke. You just don't see the smoke. Anytime you have combustion, you have smoke. Buses smoke more than cars because they burn diesel, and most people see the bus smoke because they are directly behind the bus. You want to know about blue smoke."

"Wyoming is indeed a small town on a long street."

"Generally speaking, there are three kinds of smoke from a diesel engine: black, blue, and white. Black smoke is most common, and it indicates incomplete fuel combustion. If a bus smokes, it's most likely

101

to be black smoke because most of the buses on the road are old. White smoke is not uncommon, but I don't see a lot of it. White smoke means the fuel is not burning properly. Blue smoke, the kind you are asking about, means your engine is burning oil. The most likely reason is that you have worn piston rings or a faulty valve system. That leaks oil into the diesel, and you get the blue smoke. All smoke comes and goes unless there is a real problem. Let me revise that; if a bus is spewing a lot of smoke, any color, it goes into the shop for repair. White smoke and blue smoke come and go. If the smoke persists, the bus goes into the shop. Replacing the piston rings is expensive, so you only do it if you absolutely, positively, have to."

"I know this is a crazy question . . ."

"You want to know if you can make a bus smoke. Like I said, all of Wyoming . . .

". . . is a small town. I'm getting used to it."

"Yes, you can make a bus smoke. Thinking like a bad person, if I wanted to make a bus smoke, I'd get something like a syringe or a small cooking baster and fill it with some kind of low-heat sensitive liquid. You might even be able to find that kind of liquid in a magic shop. You would just walk around to the back of the bus and squirt it into the exhaust pipe. Even if the bus was off, the pipe would still be hot enough to vaporize the liquid into blue smoke. Lots of liquid, lots of blue smoke."

"Or a more sophisticated liquid."

"Maybe. Maybe not. I'm an expert on buses, not smoke."

"How much smoke would it take to set off a fire alarm?"

"Not a lot. The problem isn't the smoke itself. I mean, the smoke you can see. There are a lot of other things in smoke that affect the fire alarm. The threshold for setting the alarm off is low because of insurance. You don't want people suing the bus company because they claim their shortness of breath comes from being in a smoky bus terminal."

"So having the alarm go off if a bus is smoking is not unusual."

"No. Just as likely the bus driver or the terminal manager would see the smoke and pull the alarm."

"Or someone on the bus."

"Possibly."

"So it's perfectly reasonable for a bus to smoke. And blue smoke does not indicate much. And having a fire alarm go off because of smoke in a terminal is not unusual either."

"Yes, and sorry. I was hoping I could help you crack the case."

Noonan didn't say anything but kept writing in his notebook. Finally, he looked up. "Just one more thing," Noonan said as he turned to go. "You are an unabashed Viking." He pointed at the ceramic map of Norway and the oversized print of Thorstein Skevla and Skjervald Skrukka. "But your first name is *Nels*. That's Swedish. How did that happen?"

"My father married beneath his station; my mother was Swedish."

CHAPTER 28

Joshua Three Trees was split on his feelings for Las Vegas. On the downside, it was not Wyoming. Nothing like Wyoming. A long way from Wyoming. Was not wide open like Wyoming and had more people in a single block than Wyoming had at the height of tourist season statewide. On the upside, this was where the money was. The big money.

The three of them met in a clothing optional rent-by-the-hour sauna out on the desert. What happens in Vegas stays in Vegas was the plan, and being without clothes had nothing to do with sex. It had to do with wires. Each of them trusted the other, but such was not the case up the administrative food chain of their respective coconspirators, particularly when it came to Three Trees. His partners had spent too much time watching cops and robbers show. But that was fine with Three Trees. It was a good idea to be over safe. He was only going to be doing one big money transaction in his life, and this was it. On his end, the transfer of money was legal, legitimate, and confirmed by the legal beagles in the casino consortium.

He wasn't facing any legal consequences.

She was.

But she knew exactly what she was doing.

She had set the whole plan in motion. Made the contact in Las Vegas. Made the contact with Three Trees. She was the one taking the risk. But it didn't matter because she would be long gone when the scheme would be revealed. But then again, it stood a very good chance of being a silent robbery, one where the insurance companies quietly paid off rather than risk the publicity. So, at the end of the day, it just might be a nonrobbery event. Three Trees liked that idea. So did the fat man from the casino consortium.

"There is just one more shoe to fall," she told the two. "After the detective talks to our man in Casper, we will move. Quickly. I figure we will have about thirty-six free hours. The money has to be paid and transferred in that window. When your check has cleared, the papers will be signed over."

"Why thirty-six hours?" the fat man asked.

"The key to success here is chaos," she said. "We have to keep John Law struggling to figure out what is happening. Everyone will eventually figure out what has happened, but by then it will be too late. The money will have been transferred and buried. The paperwork will have been filed legally, and then"—she pointed to the fat man—"your consortium will be the only game in town."

"And that's the way we like it," the fat man said and slopped water on his face.

CHAPTER 29

Undoubtedly the best-known drink in the world, both in the East and in the West, is the martini. It can be made with gin or, as James Bond prefers it, with vodka, "shaken, not stirred." Depending on whom you ask—and when—the perfect martini is served straight in a cocktail glass with an olive or lemon twist. Straight or on the rocks, your choice. But the mix ratio is important. The IBA, International Bartenders Association, lists the current standard as 6:2, gin and vermouth. But these numbers had changed over the years. During Prohibition when you weren't supposed to be drinking at all, the ratio was 3:1. When liquor became legal and America went to war, 4:1. As the years went on, the denominator stayed the same but the numerator went to six, eight, twelve, fifteen, and even as high as fifty or one hundred. Per playwright Noël Coward, "A perfect Martini should be made by filling a glass with gin, then waving it in the general direction of Italy."

The reason one salutes Italy, even though there may not be as much as a hint of vermouth in the cocktail glass, is because Italy is the home of this fortified wine, which is flavored with a variety of roots, barks, flowers, seeds, herbs, and spices. While fortified wines have been around for a millennium, the most popular vermouth comes from Torino, Italy, where it has been marketed under the label Martini & Rossi since 1863. In fact, it is the *Martini* of *Martini & Rossi* that gives the drink its name.

Ernest Hemingway, Humphrey Bogart, and James Bond have made the martini a household name in America, but in Italy, the names are a comedic punch line. When a businessman wished to indicate that *everyone* was involved in some enterprise, the salesman would say that the investors had included family members of the Sabatini, Ferraro, Martini, and Rossi. When shell corporations were established in Italy to hide foreign investment, the names Martini and Rossi often appeared as corporate directors.

Such was the case of the Stupinigi Corporation of Torino. Established at the same time as the Nimerigar, it had a threefold purpose. First, since it was established in Italy, it was legal for Italians to invest Italian money in the corporation. The currency laws in Italy, archaic as they are, only allowed a certain amount of cash to be exported out of the country. To dodge the restriction, rich Italians invested in Italian companies that had foreign investments. As long as those foreign investments did not convert to cash within a set time period—which varied with each election—the money could legally leave the country. The Stupinigi Corporation, on paper, had five corporate directors. Two of them, however, were Giuseppe Martini and Geraldo Rossi. Then there was a Lorenzo Furbo, a bona fide Italian lawyer whose law firm was a post-office address only. With three directors of the five, the company was legitimately Italian. The other directors were a Nathaniel Three Trees of Wyoming and Karen Hutchinson of Las Vegas.

The Stupinigi Corporation directors met quarterly, as required by Italian law, and filed corporate papers as required by Italian law. Its asset base began with the acquisition of a defunct railroad-and-mining conglomerate on the western slopes of the Laramie Mountains and the adjacent flatlands advancing on the miniscule—miniscule by Italian standards—community of Colter, Wyoming. The corporation was also leaping through US Bureau of Land Management hoops and State of Wyoming requirements to acquire land in the general area of the three counties that included Washakie, Bridger, and Colter.

To those in the know in the three counties, the Stupinigi Corporation was simply a scam by some clever Italian lawyer. These pie-in-the-sky schemes were a dime a dozen. A horde of mining conglomerates, railroad enterprises, homesteads, fracking companies, and dude ranches had come and gone. The Stupinigi was just another one. When the casino concept collapsed under its own weight, the Stupinigi Corporation would quietly sell out to some other pie-in-the-sky shyster, and the process would begin again.

The only difference between the Stupinigi Corporation and those who had come before was this company had a local lawyer, Harold Bodacious. He was headquartered out of his own office in Colter where he specialized in anything that made money. To have Harold Bodacious represent you meant one of two things: you were sleazy and needed representation for an underhanded enterprise or needed a connection for an underhanded enterprise. Either way, everyone knew a shoe was going to drop. When and where, no one knew because if Harold Bodacious was involved, something just might happen.

CHAPTER 30

Historically speaking, and considering his knowledge of Alaskan history because of his wife, Noonan was not so sure he was looking forward to visiting Cheyenne. It was, after all, the epicenter of the Johnson County War, and smack-dab in the center of the Johnson County War was Frank M. Canton, cowboy and hired assassin.

Canton had a reputation as a cold-blooded killer while working as a peace officer in Oklahoma and Wyoming before he went to Alaska to let things cool down in the lower states and territories. He had been a criminal in Texas under the name of Joe Horner and had killed at least one man legally, Bill Dunn, in the line of duty when he was a lawman in Pawnee, Oklahoma, in November 1894. Dunn, a criminal, rode into town to kill Canton and, in a classic good-guy-versus-bad-guy confrontation, hid in the doorway of a butcher shop until Canton came out of a restaurant where he had been serving subpoenas. Canton walked up the plank sidewalk, his hands in his pockets because it was a brisk day.

But he was armed with a Colt .45.

Dunn stepped out into the open and yelled, "Frank Canton. I've got it in for you."

Canton claimed he saw "murder in [Dunn's] eyes" and Dunn's hand on his gun.

Canton was fast. He snatched his Colt from a clip on his waistband and fired at the outlaw point-blank range. The slug struck Dunn in the forehead before the man had a chance to fire, and he went down heavily still "working the trigger finger of his right hand." A grand jury declared this to be a case of "plainly justifiable homicide."

The saga of Frank Canton in Alaska was short and painful. Constantly short of cash because the government was slow to pay, he had to pay many of his expenses out of his own pocket. These expenses were necessary because he could find no one in Circle who was willing to feed prisoners at the rate of three dollars a day, and the federal wage for being a jail guard was so low there were no takers. Even when Canton was paid, the money was inadequate for his upkeep. "It has been a hardship on me to discharge the duties of the office as I have no funds at my command"—Canton wrote his superior—"and have been compelled to borrow money to meet expenses."

Canton never did receive any compensation from his superior. Then he was dismissed. The year before he had come to Alaska he had been accused of submitting fraudulent expense claims while he had been in Oklahoma. The wheels of justice move slowly, but they did move, and Canton was left in Alaska and broke. He had to borrow from a friend to pay for a steamship ticket to Seattle.

His life in the lower states and territories was a lot more sordid. Born Josiah Horner in 1849, he spent his early years drifting, robbing banks, and rustling cattle. In 1874 he got into a gunfight with some buffalo soldiers, killing one. Three years later he was arrested for robbing a bank in Comanche, Texas. He escaped while still a prisoner and moved to Nebraska where he changed his name to Frank M. Canton.

After a vain attempt to walk the straight and narrow path, he ended up in Johnson County, Wyoming, working for the Wyoming Stock Growers Association as a "detective." For "detective," Noonan and historians read "killer." The euphemism in those days was "regulator." And, at the same time, he was working as US deputy marshal.

On April 9, 1892, in a scene that would be relived in all manner of Western movies for next century, Canton and a body of regulators descended upon the KC Ranch. Two men outside were captured right away and another one killed. Nate Champion, the target of the raid, holed up inside the K C ranch house held off the regulators for most of the day. Champion killed at least four regulators and wounded several others. Canton, finally tired of being forced to wait Champion out, set the house on fire. When Champion came out of the house, gun blazing, he was shot twenty-eight times. A few days later, the table was turned. Some of Champion's friends and a sheriff descended on the regulators at the TA Ranch, and a gun battle ensued. Canton survived the battle but was never charged with any crime. A century later, there is a Nate Champion Statue at the entrance to the Wyoming Cowboy Hall of Fame in Buffalo, Wyoming, and Champion was in the first class of inductees. Frank M. Canton is not in the Wyoming Cowboy Hall of Fame.

Basically, the Wyoming Stock Growers Association—headquartered out of Cheyenne—was nothing more than a power grab by wealthy ranchers to drive out the smaller operations. Canton and the regulators were hired to kill or chase off the smaller operators. How involved was Canton with the actual killings? History records Canton's forces of law and order—such as they were in days when there was a US deputy marshal on one side and a sheriff on the other—lost a gripsack, which contained, according to Wikipedia, "a list of 70 [Johnson] County residents to be either shot or hanged, and a contract to pay [the Regulators] $5 a day plus a bonus of $50 for every rustler, real or alleged they killed."

After the Johnson County War, Canton moved to Oklahoma where he continued to work as a US deputy marshal and later for Isaac "Hanging Judge" Parker with such Western legends as Heck Thomas, Chris Madson, Bill Tilghman, and the man who would become the model for "The Lone Ranger," Bass Reeves.

All in all, Canton had lived a speckled life, and Noonan, a lifelong advocate of law and order, found Canton to be historically interesting but legally repulsive at the same time. Further, the Johnson County Wars were not that long in the past, and, in Wyoming, as Chloe Fetterman had so accurately stated, the Sand Creek Massacre was "yesterday."

Casper was not that large by North Carolina standards—sixty thousand—so Noonan had no trouble finding the psychiatric facility. He also had no problem meeting with Harrison Day Three as long as he had his *loyer* there. That was what the *loyer* said, not Harrison Day Three. Noonan was lucky that the *loyer* was there because she was the only person in the room answering questions. Harrison Day Three was all over the psychological map.

The FBI was recording his thoughts.

He was being sent to Hawaii as part of the witness protection program.

The Pope had given him a new name.

He had a fortune that the State of Wyoming was keeping for itself.

He had been assaulted twenty-eight times in the last week at the psychiatric facility.

The *loyer* was most apologetic. "Sorry you wasted the four hours driving here from Washakie," she said. "Mr. Harrison has been this way since he checked himself in here."

Noonan was taken by surprise. "He checked himself in?"

"Yes, I thought you knew that. The police in Washakie knew it. There was nothing to hold him on. They tried to get a court order but failed. Mr. Harrison agreed to be checked in. Why, I do not know. He's not here under a court order."

"So he can get out at any time?"

"That's the law."

"Then why are you here?"

"There is a murder involved, and Mr. Harrison is a destitute suspect. He's entitled to legal representation."

"As I understand what you said, you only represent him with regard to the case of murder, not being held here."

"Correct. I have no say whether he comes or goes from here. I only handle the paperwork for the murder charge."

"And there has been no murder charge."

"Not as far as I know."

"You are correct; this was a wasted trip."

"Sorry."

Noonan shrugged. "That's OK. I've always wanted to visit Rawlins."

"To see the skin shoes, right?"

"How did you know that?"

"Everyone in law enforcement who comes to Casper finds an excuse to go to Rawlins. What else would they do in a town of ten thousand in the middle of nowhere?"

"You read me like a book."

The *loyer* pulled out a sheet of paper and handed it to Noonan. "Leave me your cell phone just in case Mr. Harrison becomes lucid. Not that I believe that is going to happen in your lifetime, but you never know."

"I'm going to spend the night in Rawlins," Noonan said. "If anything happens, let me know. I have to come back through Casper to get to Bridger."

CHAPTER 31

"Are you sure?" she asked.

"He's come and gone. Drove from Casper this morning."

"You weren't following him, were you? That would be risky."

"Naw, I'm not that stupid. Kept an eye on the *loyer*. When she went to the facility, I followed. The bearded guy came out, got in a Washakie cop car, and headed out."

"West?"

"Yup. I'm betting he's headed to Rawlins."

"Every cop who comes to Wyoming goes to Rawlins."

"It's time for our bird to fly. He's done his job. Give the bearded guy an hour. That will make a cell-phone call hard. Make sure the *loyer* doesn't know his client is in the wind."

"That will not be a problem. The PD is up to his earlobes in freebies. It will be days before she knows her client is on the dodge."

CHAPTER 32

If you were in law enforcement and you knew your history, Rawlins was on your bucket list. It was the final resting place, so to speak, of one of the most unusual outlaws—and episodes—of the West. Noonan never expected to be in the West, but now he was here; how could he resist a trip to Rawlins?

He couldn't.

So he didn't.

Even a century and a half after the saga of "Big Nose George" Parrott, Rawlins was still a flyspeck of civilization. It had been established in the 1870s as a way station for the Union Pacific Railroad as it stretched across the Great Plains toward California. Since it was a way station, it saw a century of celebrities pass through the train depot—until planes stole the traffic away. Another of those oddities of Wyoming—the town was named for General John A. Rawlins, chief of staff of the US Army. In 1867, while on patrol and thirsty, he and a detachment of scouts discovered the springs around which the community was founded. "If anything is ever named after me," Rawlins reportedly stated as he was drinking the elixir, "I hope it will be a spring of water." He didn't say this was the spring he wanted named after him or, for that matter, if he would have preferred another liquid refreshment, whichever is lost to the sands of time. But the spring was named Rawlins Spring, and when a community grew up around the water source, its name was shortened to Rawlins.

Rawlins's claim to fame in the annals of law enforcement came in 1878 when a band of violent men came up with a bone-chilling crime. In order to rob the Union Pacific Railroad, they loosened the track so the train would derail. Then they would sift through the wreckage for loot. They were able to manipulate the rail loose from the crossties, but luck was not with them. As they stood in the bushes waiting for the carnage, the loosened rail was discovered by a section crew on a handrail car. While some of the crew was repairing the track, the handrail cart was sent down the track to stop the oncoming train. After the train was stopped, a small posse was sent out to chase down the criminals. Unfortunately for the posse, the criminals were run to earth at Rattlesnake Canyon in Elk Mountain where the outlaws slaughtered every member of the posse.

This act of murder on top of the attempt to derail a train and kill dozens of innocent travelers set off a wave of anger in the newly-formed territory of Wyoming. A walloping reward of $10,000 was offered for the capture of criminals. One of the gang was killed the next month robbing the Black Hills Stage Line and a second, Dutch Charlie, was captured alive. But he did not stay that way long. On his way back to Rawlins, the train was stopped in Carbon, about fifty miles from Rawlins, and Dutch Charlie was unceremoniously lynched from a telegraph pole.

"Big Nose George" Parrot almost suffered the same fate. He took to drinking and boasting—in that order—in Miles City, Montana, and a telegram was sent to the Carbon County sheriff who came north and arrested Parrot. Miles City, interestingly, was named because the local commander, General Nelson Miles, declared that "whiskey caused him more trouble than the Indians." So, in the spring of 1877, he evicted the liquor sellers. The liquor dealers left the small community of Tongue River Cantonment and established their own town where liquor could be sold—two miles away. Over the years, Tongue River Cantonment disappeared, and, predictably, Miles City remained—a testament to the ability of whiskey to survive in even the harshest environment of the American West.

Parrot made it as far as Carbon where, as was expected, he was greeted by a contingent of vigilantes who wished to make him two of two. Parrot was clearly a better negotiator than Dutch Charlie because he escaped the noose by promising to tell all if he were to make it to Rawlins alive. Parrot made it back to Rawlins where he told a wild tale of the gang having been led by Jesse and Frank James. This was hard to believe as Wyoming was far from the haunts of the James brothers in Missouri. Telling all did not help Parrot. He was sentenced to hang on April 2, 1881.

All seemed to be going well in the law-abiding town of Rawlins until March 22, when Parrot attacked his jailer and tried to escape. He was only stopped when the jailer's wife pulled a gun on Parrot and forced him back into his cell. As far as the vigilantes were concerned, one escape attempt was one too many, and "Big Nose George" was dragged from his cell and strung up on a convenient telegraph pole. Twice the hanging was botched, but finally Parrott was killed.

In an attempt to discover what had made him a criminal, two local doctors claimed the body to extract the brain for scientific study. A portion of Parrot's skull was removed and the brain examined. Medical history does not record any aberration in Parrot's brain that would have led to his criminality. One of the doctors made a death mask of Parrot and sent skin from the outlaw's thigh and chest to a tannery in Denver with instructions to make a make a pair of shoes and a medicine bag. Legend has it that he was displeased with the shoes because the nipples of "Big Nose George" were not visible. The doctor, John Eugene Osborne, later became the third governor of Wyoming, 1893–95, and wore the shoes made of "Big Nose George" at his inauguration.

But the tale of "Big Nose George" did not stop there. Dr. Osborne kept the corpse of Parrot for more than a year while he dissected more and more of it. He kept the cadaver in a whiskey barrel filled with salt water and finally buried it behind the home of the doctor who had removed Parrot's brain. There the mutilated carcass remained until the 1950s when it was uncovered during construction by a crew digging a basement for a new building. Any doubts as to the identity of the bones were erased when the piece of cranium from the skull of "Big Nose George" that had been removed by the two doctors was found. For the previous seven decades, it had been in the possession of Lillian Heath who had been a fifteen-year-old medical apprentice at the time of Parrot's demise. She had subsequently gone on to become the first female doctor in Wyoming. In the intervening seventy years, she had used Parrot's skullcap as both a penholder and doorstop while her husband had used it as an ashtray.

While the shackles "Big Nose George" was wearing on the day he was hung and the telltale skullcap are on display in the Union Pacific Museum in Omaha, Nebraska, Parrot's death mask and skin shoes are on display in the Rawlins Museum. As long as Noonan was in Wyoming, a state he had never intended to visit, he felt it was his sworn duty as a lawman to at least take a look at the artifacts.

"What you needed were seven-league boots," Noonan said to himself silently as he looked the skin shoes, "and now, I've seen a soul of the damned" as he chuckled at his own pun.

CHAPTER 33

Few would argue the namesake of Bridger, Wyoming, has his fingerprints all over the history of the state. James Felix Bridger was orphaned at a young age and spent his early years as an apprentice to a blacksmith. At eighteen he jumped at the chance to get out of the blacksmithing business and add adventure to his life. He joined the General William Ashley Upper Missouri Expedition and became a mountain man and trapper in the fur-trading business. He is, unfortunately, best known today as one of the two men who left Hugh Glass to die after a ferocious bear attack. The survival of Hugh Glass has been seared into the public psyche by the movie *The Revenant*. Glass swore to kill the two men who had abandoned him but forgave Bridger because of Bridger's age at the time. Glass never killed the other man, John Fitzgerald, because Fitzgerald was in the US Army at the time. It would have been the death penalty to kill someone in the army. All Glass could do was advise Fitzgerald to never leave the army. If he did, Glass would hunt him down and kill him. Glass was later killed by Indians, so he never got the chance to satisfy his lust for revenge.

Bridger spent the bulk of his life as a mountain man. He was one of the first white men to see what is now Yellowstone National Park and the first white man to see the Great Salt Lake—which, because of its salt content—he thought might be connected to the Pacific Ocean. He married three times, his last wife being the daughter of Chief Washakie. True to his Wyoming roots, he told tall tales with a straight face, which have become part of Wyoming legend. He has become immortal for his tales of the "petrified forest" where the "petrified birds" sang "petrified songs." How one could hear a "petrified song" remains a mystery to this day.

Buckle Bunny Lake was one of those lakes beautiful enough to get people to consider moving to Bridger. Even Noonan felt the draw of the surprisingly extensive body of water. It wasn't salt water, but, then again, if he *had* to live somewhere other than in North Carolina—and he *had* to live away from salt water—Buckle Bunny Lake would not have been a bad choice.

What surprised him was the size of the lake. North Carolina had its lakes, but in his neck of the woods near the coast, the bodies of water were called swamps. This lake had to be at least twenty miles long by ten miles wide.

"The lake has some spots a thousand feet deep," Bridger Chief of Police Austin Kernak told Noonan. "It's also unusual. We've got the continental divide all around the region," he said, pointing around the lake, "so the lake doesn't have normal drainage. We also got a lot of unusual fish in the lake. Back in the 1870s a train stalled on the tracks—when we had railroad tracks—and it had a load of fish for some hatchery out west. When the train stalled, the fish started dying. The railway people just dumped the fish into the lake. The fish apparently loved the lake and so did their offspring. Today we're loaded with fish. Are you a fisherman?"

"Sure am," Noonan replied. "I do all my fishing at the grocery store."

"Never come home empty handed," Kernak said as he laughed. "I know why you're here, but I don't know why."

"I'm just a nosey guy."

"Good enough for me, Heinz—and I know you want to be called Heinz."

"Because Wyoming is a small state."

"It ain't North Carolina. Then again, you don't have lakes like this in North Carolina."

"It's a beautiful lake; I'll grant you that."

Chief Kernak handed Noonan six sheets stapled together. "Not much here, I'm afraid. No witness to the robbery. We were alerted to the robberies by a woman who reported seeing two figures in masks with a gun. She didn't know a burglary had been committed. She was just being a good citizen calling in an open gun."

"So she didn't know there had been a burglary?"

"Nope. She called in the gun. When that happens, we lock down the school and send our people out to investigate. A few minutes later, we got calls from the coin store and jewelry store. There had been a B&E."

"They didn't have alarms?"

Kernak shook his head. "This is Wyoming, not North Carolina. And small-town Wyoming at that. Our businesses don't have alarms and security cameras."

"How much was taken?"

"Penny ante stuff. About five thousand dollars between the two businesses. Everything that was taken was counter stuff. Nothing from the safe. Neither store."

"Seems like a wasted effort."

"Druggies. Needed cash for a fix. Insurance covered the loss."

"Any of the stolen merchandise consignment?

"As far as I know, all of it was consignment. Stores didn't get a dime out of it. Insurance covered the loss and repair to the windows and doors. EOS."

"EOS?"

"End of story. California term."

Noonan pulled out his notebook and flipped to a page. "The other two robberies have the perps as wearing masks. Your witness said the perps had masks. Did you see what kinds?"

"No. But she didn't call to report the masks. One of the perps had a pistol. That's what she reported."

"Having a gun in Wyoming is something you report?" Noonan was incredulous. "This is Wyoming," Noonan said with surprise clearly in his voice. "I thought everyone carried a weapon."

Kernak laughed. "We've got a few nutcases who carry guns everywhere, but seeing someone with a gun is unusual. It's also illegal. We don't want people walking the streets spinning a six-shooter on their index finger. We also don't want anyone in a bar with a gun or around a school. She saw the gun and called it in."

"The perps matched the robberies in Colter and Washakie?"

"Yes. But we only have the woman's word for it." Kernak paused for a moment. The point here is that the woman called in a gun near a school. We take guns near schools seriously."

"Can I talk to this witness?"

"Sure. I'll have her come by the office."

"What did you do after you discovered the burglary?"

"The usual. Did a sweep of the area, checked the hotels and bus station. We had roadblocks up for an hour or so, but nothing came of it."

"No one unusual was found?"

"You got it. At least no one who fit the description of the perps. Man over six feet and smaller figure, probably a woman. Not much. We've got a lot of people who fit that description."

"Any unusual folks in town?"

"The usual crowd. Some cowboys, yes," he said as Noonan started to say something, "some of them over six feet but they all had alibis if that's what you were going to ask."

"That was what I was going to ask. Who else was in town that wasn't a local?"

"Had a guy from the land office in Cheyenne, a woman from the Department of the Interior handling land transfers from the feds, a vet doing some research, and a history professor doing a book on the history of Buckle Bunny Lake. We checked them all out. All clean. The land guy from Cheyenne is part of a computerization of records for the state, the Interior woman was off on a field trip that night, the vet was at a ranch fifteen miles out of town, and the prof was out on the water when the burglary came down."

"Noonan looked at his notes. "There was a state person in Washakie when the last robbery was committed. Could it be the same man?"

"Most likely. The State of Wyoming is computerizing all its records. Land records in particular. He's been helping the counties get their records ready."

"You know him?"

"Everybody knows Darby. He's a fixture."

"Darby over six feet?"

Kernak laughed. "Two of him, yeah. No, he's about five four or five. Too short for one burglar and too tall for the other."

"Was he working anywhere near the burglaries?"

"Everything in Bridger is close to everywhere. Darby was in the county building, which is on the other side of town. Say, ten, twelve blocks away. Besides, why would he be burglarizing a coin store and a jewelry store?"

"I don't know. But he's been in two towns that had robberies. Quite a coincidence."

"You'll find a lot of people who were in all three towns on all three days. This is Wyoming. Our civil servants and the feds do a lot of travel. We like it that way. Makes it personal."

"And puts money into the local economy."

"Our tax dollars at work." Kernak smiled. "Darby's got a girlfriend in town, so he doesn't pump money into the local economy when he comes here."

"Directly."

"Not directly. No."

"Is his girlfriend five feet tall?"

"As a matter of fact, yes. She's the one who reported the couple in the masks."

"Can I talk to her?"

"I'll see what I can do."

Noonan was about to leave and then had one more question. "Just another question: Are there any Harrison families around here?"

The chief laughed. "None that are dead if that's what you mean. We've checked. There is no link between any of them and the two—one living and one dead—in Washakie."

"Anything unusual about the Nimerigar here in Colter?"

"Unusual? Fighting to get title to fifty thousand acres of rattlesnake land is unusual. Not really. Word is they're working with an Italian land company over some land deal."

"Just a second," Noonan said as he plowed through his notebook. He finally found the page he was looking for. "Maybe the Stupinigi Corporation?"

"Sounds like it. I don't speak Italian, so I don't know. It has a lawyer in Colter. If I had any questions, I'd ask him."

"Are there any Nimerigar here in Bridger?"

"There are Nimerigar in Bridger, Colter, and Washakie. Didn't you talk with the Nimerigar in Washakie?"

"Sort of."

"Well, you'll get the same response here. A lot of lore and legend and not a dime's worth of information. Do you really want to talk with a Nimerigar person?"

"Yes. Can you arrange it?"

"Done. Here's an address. I'll make the call. He'll talk, but you won't get anything out him. Best of luck. And I mean it."

CHAPTER 34

"Iron-Man, whose real name in Shoshone was *Wihindaibo*, was the father of all white men, men like you, and he lived in the middle of a big sea."

"How interesting," Noonan said. "But I'm here to ask a few questions about the Nimerigar and the land . . ."

Bozheena, who had once been Jerry Hardesty but who changed his name to Buffalo in Shoshone, waved Noonan quiet with a waggle of the right index finger.

"Wolf, who was the father of all Indians lived in the ground, under the ground. One day Wolf went to visit Iron-Man. But Iron-Man would not meet with Wolf because Iron-Man owned all the earth. He did not want to share. So Iron-Man locked himself in his home. But Wolf was strong and blew down Iron-Man's door with a breath."

Noonan looked at his notes and tried to speak, but Bozheena stopped him again with another waggle of his fingers.

"The Iron-Man tried to poison Wolf with tobacco in a pipe, but Wolf smoked all the tobacco with no harm to himself. When Wolf gave Iron-Man a pipe of *kinnikkinik*, Iron-Man could not finish the pipe. And the smoke from the *kinnikkinik* filled the house of Iron-Man, and he believed he had been poisoned by Wolf. So Iron-Man caused the wind to blow mightily, and it caused his house to shake so badly he ran outside and began to freeze. To keep him alive Wolf laid Iron-Man in the sun."

"That's not exactly how the legend goes," Noonan tried to cut in, but Bozheena would not stop talking.

"Then Wolf showed his power by shooting an arrow into the sun, and the world went dark. Iron-Man was very frightened and began running around and into things. Wolf feared Iron-Man would hurt himself, so Wolf brought back the sun. But still, Iron-Man was intent on defeating Wolf. Iron-Wolf challenged Wolf to a gun-making contest. But Wolf was faster than Iron-Man. Wolf made more guns than Iron-Man in the same amount of time. So Wolf won."

Bozheena fell silent.

"I'm not from around here," Noonan said slowly. "So I'm not that familiar with the local customs. Am I to interpret something from the story you just told?"

"Just as Wolf defeated Iron-Man at the beginning of time, so shall the Nimerigar defeat the Iron-Man again. The sun must be blotted out before it can return and give life to all. At the beginning of time, Wolf and Iron-Man made guns in a contest. The Nimerigar do not make guns of steel and powder but of ink and paper, the guns the white used to steal Nimerigar land at the beginning of our time. The Nimerigar will defeat the white man in this age as Wolf overcame Iron-Man at the beginning of time."

"Fine, can you give me any specifics about how the land deal will make the Nimerigar wealthy"—Noonan paused—"and defeat the white man?"

"Our Arapahoe brothers and sisters tell of *Nihancan*. He is a spider trickster who shapes the world as he goes. The whites would call him a troublemaker, a violent troublemaker. Some Arapahoe say *Nihancan* is the white man, someone who came with false promises, a crazy man and a fool. The world was born of Iron-Man and Wolf, but it moves forward. *Nihancan* is ever present. The world has many tricksters but none as devious as *Nihancan*. He is the cleverest of all."

"Clever enough to pull off a murder?"

Murder was the only word that got a rise out of *Bozheena*.

"Wolf did not kill Iron-Man. Wolf saved Iron-Man. *Nihancan* is a trickster. He is clever in his ways. *Clever* means he does not play the fool. Once upon a time *Nihancan* came upon a dwarf trying to make an arrow out of a mighty tree. *Nihancan* doubted the dwarf could make an arrow out of such a mighty tree, so he laughed at the dwarf. The dwarf became angry, and when the arrow was made, shot it at *Nihancan*. *Nihancan* ran for his life but no matter which direction he took, the arrow followed. Finally, *Nihancan* threw himself onto the ground to avoid being killed by the arrow. But the arrow hit him and buried him, to up to his neck. The dwarf helped him out of the ground and ministered to his wounds. *Nihancan* never forgot the power of the dwarf."

"Am I supposed to see the white man in these allegories?"

"Allegory is a white man's word. The Nimerigar know there is no past and no future. What the white man calls the future is simply the extension of the present, which is the result of the past. All that was will be again. Legends do not die; they are simply reborn."

"So the Nimerigar will move into the future with trickiness?"

"The Nimerigar are the future that was stolen in the past. The past will be relived in the future. The present is just waiting for the future to occur."

CHAPTER 35

Heinz Noonan had a nose. Nose, in this case, was not a reference to his proboscis. Nor was it a hint his olfactory sense was superior to others of his species. In that sense, excusing the pun, he was not Hercule Poirot. Rather, it was allusion to a hint of the unseen. It could be said of a football player, head down, churning through a wall of defenders that his extra effort was because he could "smell the goal line." The player did not actually *smell* the goal line, but he knew it was there. Exactly where it was. In a battle, warriors can smell victory. There is also the sweet scent of success along with other metaphoric smells.

Noonan's olfactory senses worked in reverse. He could not smell the positive, only the negative. Fragrance had no place in his hall of smells. Politics had an unmistakable stench. Incompetence was not nearly as overpowering, but it was still discernable in a field of roses. Duplicity was an evasive smell. More accurately, it was inconsistent. The mephitises of politics and incompetence was both pervasive and consistent. It did not ameliorate. It was also elusive—detectable for an instant and then gone.

Sandra Trucco was a cipher. Even for a man as seasoned as Noonan, Trucco was an anomaly. She was a fifty-year-old who looked thirty, had pose unexpected for a small town in Wyoming, spoke a sophisticated English with an accent that was not local. She pulsed street smart, and

128

before she even sat down, Noonan picked up the miasma of deceit. But it wasn't the scent of duplicity from a criminal—rather, the wafting of misdirection. This woman was a pro.

"I was told you wanted to see me," Trucco said, without missing a beat. She was clearly used to cops. She had the cageyness of a street person, to reveal only that which was necessary and not an iota more. Noonan read her perfectly. He was not going to get anything useful out of this woman. He was pretty sure she read him the same way. But whatever it was that was going on, she was part of it. Most likely the heart of it.

"I'd like to talk with you about the robberies of the coin shop and jewelry store here in Bridger."

She reacted like a pro, a bona fide member of the DKN (Don't know Nuthin') Club. "Oh, I heard there'd been some criminal activity, but I don't know anything about it."

"Didn't you report a crime?" Noonan made a show of looking at his notes, as if he was checking his facts, Miss Trucco?

"A crime?" This woman was a pro. "No. I only reported a man with a gun. I don't know if that's a crime. I mean, this is Wyoming."

"You're not from here?"

"I live here, if that's what you're asking."

"Not really. You just said, 'this is Wyoming' as if you lived somewhere else."

"I came from somewhere else, but I live here now. What does that have to do with the man with a gun?"

"It was a man?" Noonan made a phony effort of looking his notes. "What I have you saying was it was a pair wearing masks."

"Yes, there were two of them. One tall and the other one small. It looked like they were wearing masks. I didn't recognize them. They must have been out-of-town people."

"But you did see masks?"

"Sort of. The two were wearing some kinds of masks, but they were not looking at me. What I saw was the gun?"

"You saw a gun? Big? Small?"

"I don't know guns. It was a pistol. A handgun."

"You live in Wyoming, and you don't know a gun when you see it?"

129

"Actually, we call it a firearm. It was a ways away. If it had been closer, I could have given you a caliber."

"Which of the two was carrying the firearm?" Noonan accented the word *firearm*.

"The tall one. The man."

"How do you know he was a man?"

"He walked like a man. It could have been a woman, but I'd guess it was a man."

"And the other person was a woman?"

"She walked like a woman. It could have been a man."

"But you saw the firearm and called it in."

"Called the police, yes."

"Then you went to work?"

"Directly. At the hospital. My shift starts at nine a.m."

"What do you do at the hospital?"

"A better question is what I don't do. I rove, do everything but medical procedures. Bridger General is small, so we all do everything: intake, supplies, ordering, janitorial, whatever."

"So you just went to work? You called in the gun and went to work?"

"That's correct."

"Didn't you say you saw the gun was close to a school?"

"Please. I saw the gun a block from the school. That's an automatic red flag for the police."

"How do you know that?"

"It was in the newspaper. Along with the story about the burglaries. All I saw was the man with the gun, and I reported it. Then I went to work."

Noonan clearly wasn't going to get anything out of this woman. The best he could do was throw her a curve and see what happened. "Why do you think the man was carrying the gun? After all, if the two had just committed a burglary, why would they need to be carrying a gun?"

Trucco didn't bat an eye. "Snakes. Wyoming is loaded with them. If the man and woman had just crawled out of the jewelry store, they would have had to have had the firearm ready in case they encountered a snake. I just happened to see them before they put it away."

"If it was burglary, why wear masks?"

"It was close to nine a.m., opening hours for stores. They were probably worried the store owner would be back before they were finished robbing the place. That's my guess."

She was good, and Noonan didn't have a curve ball left to throw.

"Is that all?" she asked after a long moment of silence.

"Don't leave town," Noonan said. He then quickly added, "I may want to talk with you again."

"Not a problem. I'll be at the Bridger Hospital from nine to six."

CHAPTER 36

Joshua Three Trees got the message by text while he was driving back to Washakie. He stopped the car long enough to forward the text to the fat man who forwarded the text to the lawyer for the consortium who forwarded the text to the consortium treasurer. An hour later Three Trees got the text that $20 million had been transferred but would not be released pending approval and signatures. Three Trees smiled and stopped the car. In a single fluid motion, he fastballed the cell phone across Lake Powell. It skipped a dozen times and then disappeared into the depths. After the concentric rings reached the shoreline, the waters were calm again.

CHAPTER 37

While dealing with the casino had been relatively easy, the New York Photovoltaic Corporation was a logistical nightmare. This was, of course, to be expected. The casino had put up $20 million just to keep its hand in the game. If the Nimerigar could make all of the moving parts roll in unison, it was $20 million well spent. If not, there was still tomorrow, next year, and a decade from now. Gambling was timeless. There would always be casinos, and the key to profitability was the same as real estate: location, location, location. It was illegal to gamble in the state of Wyoming, which would make the Nimerigar properties solid gold.

If . . .

The casino was not going to be investing a dime of actual construction money until the ownership of the roadway from the interstate was secured and the water-transportation corridors from Buckle Bunny Lake were affirmed in court. But that was only a portion of the problem. Another big one was power. You could not have a casino without power. It was not power that was the problem, it was POWER! The casino was going to need a lot of long-term sustainable, dependable power—day and night, 24-7, winter and summer. Packed with gamblers or empty as the halls of Timbuktu. "If you build it, they will come," was certainly true of casinos, and the casino on Nimerigar

133

land would be available to more than ten million people within a day's drive of the casino. It would be the Las Vegas of the Badlands.

Success for the Nimerigar was a three-legged stool. One leg was the casino, and that was in play. The second was the ownership of the fifty thousand acres of land, which had been approved by the United States but was in the process of being conveyed, a bureaucratic slow boat to China. The third was the combined, consistent, dependable supply of water and power. The paperwork for the corridors that had been placed before the board of directors of the New York Photovoltaic Corporation was, at best, schizophrenic. On the one hand, the Nimerigar operation was their best possible opportunity to make millions. The land was free, there would be a megascale consistent client to buy the bulk of the power within a few hundred yards of the power plant, which meant that voltage leakage would be minimal, and being on Native land, there would not be as many pesky regulations to deal with.

The flip side of the coin was a bit more daunting. The photovoltaic operation would initially overprovide the power for the casino and all outside buildings. But that was only within the first eighteen to twenty-four months. As the solar field expanded to become more efficient, it would be producing more power than the casino could consume. That would force the photovoltaic corporation into the red at the worst possible time: its grant money would have been extinguished. Thus, it was critical for the corporation to have transmission corridors to get the excess power from the solar operation to, at the very least, initially, Colter and Bridger. Ownership of the roadway made power to Washakie a given. Then, over the long term, the power from the photovoltaic plant had to link to the nationwide grid of electric lines so power could be wheeled off Nimerigar land to homes and factories far from the Badlands.

The Nimerigar scheme was, at best, devious. Legal was yet another consideration. But the fact of the matter remained that it was, if nothing else, clever. It could—reasonably—be successful, but the board of directors of the New York Photovoltaic Corporation had a long-term vision. If the Nimerigar operation was successful, there were lots of Indian reservation and Native-owned lands where casinos with photovoltaic power were possible.

With an eye to a Niagara of federal-grant moneys, the New York Photovoltaic Corporation demanded an arm's length transaction. So, the Philadelphia lawyer provided a string of corporate entities that would provide cover for the corporation. This might have been called *laundering* if money had been involved. But no money was involved, just land ownership. Even more delicious, the paper trail between Nimerigar and New York twisted through Italy, and the initial corporation had a board of directors who would vanish as soon as the casino's $20 million in promise became $20 million in negotiable paper.

"We'll leave nothing behind but dust," the Philadelphia lawyer had told his colleagues. "The only thing we have to be is gone."

CHAPTER 38

Noonan's initial reaction to O'Reilly was that he, O'Reilly, was prey. God made some people predators, others prey. This did not mean one was simply fodder for the other. But it did mean that one followed the other. There was a symbiosis. The casino owner needed the gambler just as the gambler needed the casino. The casino was the predator; the gambler was the prey. At the end of the day, the predator had the money, but the gambler would be back. There would always be gamblers. There would always be casinos. There would always be predators. There would always be prey.

O'Reilly was prey.

But this did not mean he was like a crippled mouse hiding in the forest underbrush. He was more like an adolescent hyena hungering to fit into the food chain. He was cagey, not frightened.

People who were cagey had something to hide.

Noonan made a show of looking through his notebook while O'Reilly fretted at the table across from Noonan. While Noonan flicked pages, O'Reilly ran his finger around the rim of his paper coffee cup and tapped the liquid with the red plastic straw from the coffee shop. Finally, Noonan looked up.

"Mr. O'Reilly, everyone has nothing to say but good things about you."

This clearly took O'Reilly by surprise. This was probably the first time in his life he had been to a police interview. He'd never even been to traffic court; Noonan had checked. O'Reilly's legal record was as unblemished as the first snow of the season before it is sullied by ash, snowplows, and debris blown in from Colorado. Or Montana. He had not even been to court over any land issues. He was virginal. Now, to have a law-enforcement officer say nice things about him, well, it was clearly a surprise.

He didn't know what to say. So, he stayed true to the advice every father gives his child: when you don't know what to say, don't say anything.

Noonan smiled. "No reason to say anything, Mr. O'Reilly. I was just passing along an observation. The real reason I wanted to talk to you was because you were one of the few people who were in Washakie and Bridger on the days of the robberies."

"I've been in and out of those cities along with a lot of other ones lately. I guess it was just coincidence I happened to be in Bridger and Washakie on those days. We, that is, the State of Wyoming, is computerizing all its paper land records, so I am, quite literally, everywhere all the time."

"But you are based out of Cheyenne, right?"

"Yes, at the head office."

"But you were in the two cities on the days of robberies. Do you know about the robberies?"

"I read the papers. We are a small state."

"So you know the people who were robbed?"

"I know who they are. It's not as if we are friends. I would recognize them on the street, but that's as far as it goes."

"You know about the murder in Washakie, I guess."

"I know about it. Everyone does. But I don't remember reading about it in the paper."

"I don't think it has made the newspaper yet. But you don't know anything about the Harrisons?"

"Why should I?"

"You were all in the Frank M. Canton Hotel together at the same time. I thought you might have run across each other."

"I could have, in the hallway or the entryway. But since I don't know what they looked like, I can't say for certain I did speak with them."

137

"Or the restaurant?"

"The Frank M. Canton Hotel does not have a restaurant."

"Well, then, in any restaurant?"

"Maybe. But I don't know what they looked like, so I don't know."

"There aren't that many visitors to Washakie. Surely you must have seen some out-of-towners in your days here in Washakie."

"If I did, I don't remember them. No one ever talks to me when I come to town." He gave a weak smile. "I'm kind of like wallpaper."

"Not true, Mr. O'Reilly. Everyone says you are the man of the hour! You are the point of the spear in the State of Wyoming's computerization program. You are the one who is smoothing the transition from the past to the future. That makes you the man of the hour, not wallpaper."

O'Reilly was clearly taken by surprise, and from the look on his face, he was flattered.

"Well, I'm just doing my job."

"Indeed you are. No one has a bad thing to say about you. Now, as to these robberies, did you see or hear anything unusual on the robbery days?"

"They were just regular days, like all the other ones."

"Actually, not so much." Noonan ruffled through some pages for show. "According to witnesses, you didn't stay in a hotel in Bridger; can I ask where you did stay when you were in Bridger?"

"Mr. Noonan, . . ."

"Heinz."

"Heinz. We are a small state. I find it hard to believe you don't know. You interviewed my girlfriend. When I'm in Bridger, I stay with her. The morning of the burglary, we both went to work. I went to the county courthouse, and she went to the hospital."

"How did you know it was a burglary?" Noonan pounced.

O'Reilly was nonplused.

"It was in the paper. Even if it didn't use the word *burglary*, everyone knows it wasn't a robbery. I'm not in law enforcement, so I don't know the exact difference. Either way, the two stores had property stolen."

"So you don't know anything about the robberies, any of them?"

"I know they happened. I know they happened while I was in town. In Bridger and Washakie, I was in the county courthouse when the robberies occurred. You can check on it if you want to. In Bridger, I got to work at nine a.m. So did my girlfriend. She called in the man with the gun near the school. I got to the county courthouse just as the registrar was on her way out. She had a child in school and wanted to make sure the kid was OK. I passed her on my way in."

"Was anyone else in the courthouse?"

"Well, yeah. I think two or three people had kids in school, and they left. But there were still about five people in the courthouse. We weren't all in the same office, but we were all in the same building. Besides, why do you care? The robberies happened before I got to work. Before my girlfriend got to work."

"Because no one's found the burglars or the loot. Don't you think that's kind of strange? A tall man and short woman with loot who simply disappear in a town this size?"

"Well, it happened. How, I don't know. Maybe they got in a car and drove away."

"There were roadblocks on the highway in both directions."

"Then they were long gone by the time the roadblocks went up. I don't know. And I really don't care. The only reason you're talking to me is because I happened to be in the two cities when two similar robberies took place. I'm not stupid. I read the newspapers. In both Washakie and here in Bridger, I was in the county courthouse helping with the computerization of land records when the robberies occurred. You can check with staff and verify I was there. In Colter, and I know you haven't asked about it yet, but you will because it fits the pattern, as you law-enforcement people say, I was at the Fourth of July festival. So, no, I don't have an alibi for that robbery. But I'm also not six feet tall, as you can see."

"But your girlfriend is short."

"So are half the women in Wyoming. Officer Heinz, I was with my girlfriend all night here in Bridger and got to work after the burglary. I was at the county courthouse in Washakie when that robbery happened. I'm sure I can find some credit-card receipts for things I bought at the Fourth of July fair in Colter when that robbery was happening. I don't know what else to tell you."

Noonan smiled. "Just a couple more things. What's the relationship between the Stupinigi Corporation and the Nimerigar?"

"Relationship?"

"Land. They are both into land. You're a land person. What have you heard?"

"Well, you are correct. They are both into land, as you put it. The Stupinigi Corporation bought out the rights to the old Laramie Consolidate Syndicate lands. They, the Stupinigi Corporation, filed the change of land status with the State of Wyoming. Once land, state or federal, becomes private, we, the State of Wyoming keep its status on file. I did the paperwork. But the Nimerigar land was federal, so the feds handled that paperwork. When the actual paperwork is filed, it will be filed with us. At that moment, what was the federal land becomes private land, and we record it."

O'Reilly took a breath and then continued, "Logically the two must be related because they share a lot of property line. And the Nimerigar road is across the old Laramie Consolidate Syndicate property over Cannibal Pass. So the Stupinigi Corporation has to deal with them. Or the other way around. But we're talking a mix of state, federal, and private land here. On top of that, there's the computerization project. Right now there is no state land for sale. Everyone is waiting for the computerization project to finish. The feds are a different story. But they are not part of the computerization project. They have their own system."

"But there is a link between the Stupinigi Corporation and the Nimerigar?" Noonan asked.

"They share property lines, but I haven't seen any sales or exchanges of land one way or the other. As far as federal lands are concerned, you'd have to ask the feds in Cheyenne."

There didn't seem to be anything else to ask, so Noonan said good-bye to O'Reilly.

CHAPTER 39

Harold Bodacious did not need to speak Italian to deal with the Stupinigi Corporation. He didn't have to. Lorenzo Furbo spoke perfect English. That was because Lorenzo Furbo wasn't Italian. He was a lawyer from Philadelphia who had a mistress in Torino. He had a license to practice in Italy, courtesy of the father of his mistress who needed an *of counsel* American lawyer as a link to the American banking system.

It was the same the whole world over. Money had to move to be useful. Italian money, as in cash, was not allowed to leave Italy in amounts larger than $10,000. But money into the millions could be invested in other countries as long as it went through an Italian corporation first. An Italian could not buy stock on the New York Stock Exchange, but he could buy shares in an Italian company that bought shares on the New York Stock Exchange.

Furbo was equally valuable to the Italian firm because he brought in money from the United States. In many cases, it was Russian money that needed to be "moved about" to hide its origin. This did not necessarily mean that the money came from illegal or illicit sources. It was just business money that needed to be hidden from the Russian government of Vladimir Putin. Putin and his cronies were rapacious, and if there was a dollar to be skimmed, they were there with skimmers. So Russian businesses in America kept three sets of books—books for Putin to see, books for the IRS to see, and the real books. Furbo shepherded Russian money from America through the Italian law firm that then filtered it through Italian companies that, in turn, returned the money in the form of investments in the United States. This was only possible because cash coming *into* Italy was not monitored by the Italian government, only Italian money earned in Italy. So Furbo was in the best of all possible worlds. He was arranging for Italian money to seep into the American market and, at the same time, funneling Russian money into the Italian market to be reinvested in the American market. It was all very circular—and profitable.

A not insubstantial amount of money had been invested in the Stupinigi Corporation. The Stupinigi Corporation was buying land in Wyoming on the gamble that it would become a silent partner in a casino conglomerate on Indian land. It was the best of all possible worlds. Casinos dealt in cash, which offered the Italians an added outlet to convert their euros to dollars. And it gave the Russians a way to *shampoo* their earnings. Further, as the casino was on Indian lands, there were fewer prying eyes.

Most importantly for Furbo, he was arranging side deals. One did not pollute the water that one was drinking. But if one was clever, one could walk away with a sizeable fortune by presenting options to people just as greedy. The trick was to keep yourself more than an arm's length away from the financials.

In Harold Bodacious, Furbo found a brother-in-arms. Each was as rapacious as the other, and both were as cautious as a cat on a tree branch in a windstorm in the forest at night. Thus, each were buttering the other's bread. It was going to take two to tango, and these two were the perfect partners.

CHAPTER 40

Bridger Police Chief Kernak was not surprised Noonan had gotten nothing out of O'Reilly. Kernak didn't believe there was anything to get out of O'Reilly. "Darby and his father have been fixtures in State of Wyoming circles for, oh, decades. I find it hard to believe he'd be wrapped up in robberies. Particularly, small ones." Bridger Police Child Kernak shook his head. "Frankly, I don't know why anyone would want to pull off some penny ante burglaries like these and then get seen! Really odd."

"How fast were the roadblocks up?"

"Real fast. We're small, but we're not incompetent."

"I didn't mean to imply that," Noonan said quickly.

"I didn't say you did. The general opinion of police in small towns by the big boys and girls in Cheyenne is that we are employed here because we can't find any other jobs."

"North Carolina big boys and girls have the same attitude."

"Unfortunately," Chief Kernak said, "sometimes they are right. As far as the roadblocks, they went up fast. From the other ends of the road. What I mean is the roadblocks were done by troopers driving into the area. They are pretty good at their job and were in place in a matter of minutes, maybe ten. The perps could have made it out of town before the roadblocks went up, but they'd had to have been moving fast."

"Any chance I can talk to the troopers who monitored the roadblocks?"

"Sure, but it will take about two hours to get them to come here. Do the robberies have anything to do with that murder in Washakie?"

"I don't know. But it's hard to believe there is not a connection."

While Noonan waited for the troopers, he used the electronic beast of Satan to see if there had been any change in the Harrison matter in Washakie. Chief Standing Bear told him that nothing had changed; one Harrison was still dead, and his body was in hiding. The other Harrison was still in the psychiatric facility in Casper; the Nimerigar were still spouting Shoshone riddles, and everything else was just the way it was when he had been in Washakie.

So much for things in Wyoming changing rapidly.

It took a while and a lot of phone calls for Noonan to track down the name of the company that owned the tour bus that had been smoking in the Washakie terminal. This was primarily because the tour industry was one of subcontract. The umbrella tour companies owned nothing but computers and a good name. Everything else was subcontract. And every subcontractor wanted no part of any detective from Sandersonville, North Carolina—wherever the heck Sandersonville was—calling about a smoking bus in a terminal in Washakie, Wyoming—wherever the heck Washakie was—because Washakie was not "part of the Western Wonderland Tours experience."

Further, Western Wonderland Tours was not based in Wyoming. It was based in Orlando, Florida, with the public relations staff in Atlanta, Georgia, and the actual contact for the bus tour was in Denver. The bus service was a subcontract out of Boulder, but the tour details were handled out of Colorado Springs. When Noonan finally reached the company that handled the bus subcontract, he was told any questions had to be routed through Western Wonderland Tours in Orlando. When Noonan said he only wanted to know about the mechanical condition of one particular bus, he was told "Nothing is wrong with any of our buses" and to submit any questions to Orlando.

He was able to get a promise from the booking agent in Colorado Springs to get a list of passengers on the bus if she could get approval from Orlando.

But it would take a while.

Noonan put a hopeful *emoji* face in his notebook.

It took the two troopers more than three hours to get to Bridger. By then the sun was setting, and there was no way for Noonan to make it back to Washakie for the night. So he settled for a modest but comfortable hotel—one of the two in town—and met the two troopers for dinner in the hotel restaurant.

"We don't get many out-of-state detectives," one of the troopers said, a man in his twenties. "Usually they call in."

"Well"—Noonan smiled as he spoke—"I'm a bit different. Tell me about the roadblocks."

Both men looked at each other. Then they looked at Noonan. "Nothing to tell," said the older one by a good fifteen minutes. "We got the call about the robbery at, say, nine oh five and were on the road within minutes. 'Least I was."

"Same here," replied Junior. "We were both coming from different directions and had roadblocks up within minutes."

"Did cars pass you going out of Bridger?"

"Sure," said Senior. "But we're talking one or two from my side. I passed them almost immediately, which means the passengers could not have been in Bridger at nine a.m. There were a couple of rigs with trailers and at least one school bus."

Noonan started to say something, but he was cut off, "The school bus was empty, if that's what you want to know. I radioed it in, and it was checked. The cars I passed were checked too. Just because we're in Wyoming doesn't mean we do slipshod jobs."

"I didn't mean that."

Junior spoke up, "You have to understand; this event you talk about was a big one for us. We get a call that a man with a weapon has been seen near a school with a mask. That's an automatic notification to all law enforcement. We were on our way to Bridger when the burglary APB came out. We had the town pretty much locked down within minutes. We stopped the traffic in both directions and did a car-by-car search. We got goose egg."

"You found no men over six feet?"

"Sorry, I didn't mean it that way," Junior said quickly. "Yes, we did get four or five men over six feet, but they all checked out. We searched their cars, with their permission, and found nothing. And before you ask, yes, three or four short women—at least on my side—and yes, they checked out as well."

"Same on my side," said Senior. "All totaled, we're talking about ten or twelve people we checked out. All had alibis. Three of them were from Bridger, but we had them on the road before nine a.m."

Noonan smiled and said. "Bridger is not that large, and as everyone keeps telling me, Wyoming is a very small town. How can a man over six feet with a woman at five feet that no one knows just disappear in a small town?"

"They didn't," said Junior. "They are either hiding out, or they never existed in the first place."

This took Noonan by surprise. "What do you mean *never existed in the first place*? Do you think the witness is lying?"

"I didn't mean that," Junior cut in quickly. "I know Sandra Trucco, and she's a piece of work, but I don't see what she would gain by lying. I mean, even if she was part of the robbery she'd end up with a few thousand dollars she couldn't spend in town because everyone knows how much everyone else makes. And she spent the night with her boyfriend, and he's not the criminal type. I'm sure she saw something. I'm guessing she saw a tall man and a short woman, and we all jumped to the conclusion that it was the same pair who robbed the coin stores and jewelry stores in Washakie and Colter. It was a logical leap of logic."

"What she could have seen?" asked Noonan.

Senior cut in, "Captain . . ."

"Heinz."

"That's right. I was told you like to be called Heinz."

"Wyoming is a small town on a very long street."

"Right, Heinz." He put an accent on *Heinz*. "What she saw was a gun. That I believe. She called it in. Then she said the gun was being held by a tall man. Every man in Wyoming is tall. And she said the man had a mask, but I don't know how she could have seen the mask if the burglars were running from the scene of the crime. I mean, the point of a burglary is to not be seen. But these perps had their masks on and were running away from the scene of the crime. My bet, she said she saw a tall man with a gun, and since the time was so close to the burglaries, the assumption was that these were the burglary perps."

"What about the masks?"

Junior sighed. "People make all kinds of mistakes. I believe she saw the gun and reported it. Everything else, well, who knows?"

"So the burglars could have slipped through the roadblocks?"

Both men spoke in unison, "No way." Junior took charge of the conversation. "We checked out everyone, not just the tall men and short women. Everyone was clean. The burglars, if they existed, could not have left Bridger before we had the roadblocks up. So they either hid out in town and waited for the roads to clear or never existed at all."

The men batted around possibilities for another half hour before the troopers had to be back on the highway. After they left Noonan spent a quarter hour going over his notes. He finished his meal and turned down dessert when a waitress old enough to be his grandmother sat down across the table.

"You're that out-of-town cop looking into the Nimerigar, aren't you?"

The move took Noonan by surprise. "Not exactly. I'm here . . ."

"Oh, we all know that," she cut in. "That strange murder over in Washakie. But it's mixed up with the Nimerigar."

"Really? How do you know that?"

"The players are all the same! There's the Three Tree family, Sandra Trucco, and Darby O'Reilly. They're all doing something strange, and then this dead body pops up. Or this dead body doesn't pop up. A lot of blood but no body."

"That all true," said Noonan cautiously, "but how are they all connected?"

"A casino! I thought you knew that. The Nimerigar have cut a deal with a casino in Las Vegas."

"How do you know that?"

"Everybody knows it. Sandra and Three Trees make trips there ever two or three weeks. They don't have the money to gamble, so it's got to be something else. Sandra's got roots in Las Vegas. Knows the right people. Or, rather, the wrong people. She knows the wrong kind of people to make a casino happen."

147

Noonan thought for a moment. "But you can't have a casino unless you've got water and power and access to the interstate. I was told none of that was going to happen."

The woman did a ppppffffftttt with her lips. "There's too much money to let it lie fallow. Darby O'Reilly could make it happen."

"How's that?"

"Oh, I don't know. He's a land man, and he could jiggle land records."

"Wouldn't that be hard to do? Those land records have paper trails back to territoryhood."

"Maybe. Maybe not. This is Wyoming, and a lot of strange things happen by the light of day as well as the full light of the moon."

Noonan was intrigued. "You think this Sandra has the connections to get a casino to come to Washakie?"

"Don't get me wrong. She's basically a good woman. Works hard at the hospital. Been here three or four years, tops. Came from Las Vegas. Then she got boyfriend, Darby O'Reilly, j-u-s-t about the time the whole deal started to come together."

"A casino has agreed to come in?" This took Noonan by surprise.

"Word is papers have been signed. By some lawyer out of Philadelphia. A Vietnam buddy of Old Man Three Trees."

"You ever see this lawyer?"

"Nope. Just know he's out of Philadelphia."

"How do you now that?"

"We're small town."

"I've heard that before."

CHAPTER 41

Benjamin Franklin once noted that diligence was the mother of good luck. Noonan hoped this was true because there was not a single thing he expected to get out of the police in Colter. Of the three robberies, this one promised to be the least productive. It had occurred on the Fourth of July, and the town was packed with outsiders. There were going to be no roadblocks. There were no security tapes. There were only two witnesses.

But due diligence was required.

Colter had been named after legendary John Colter, widely considered to be America's first mountain man. He had been on the Lewis and Clark Expedition and was the first white to see the Grand Tetons and what would become Yellowstone National Park. Historically, he is best known for a rather gruesome experience. In an "altercation" with the Blackfoot, Colter had been stripped naked and forced to run for his life. He did—with a pack of warriors behind him. After running for several miles, Colter turned on his pursuers and singled out the closest one. Colter disarmed the warrior, killed the brave with his own spear, and stole the man's blanket. He then continued his run until he came to the Madison River. Jumping into the swirling waters, he swam until he came to beaver house where he secluded himself until the pursuing warriors left. Then he walked for eleven days to a trader's fort on the Little Big Horn.

Naked.

Colter is also credited with the discovery of what was called "Colter's Hell." The year before his run to survive, he came to a remote fort with tales of geysers, mud pots, and a "stinking river." He identified the region, which quickly became known as "Colter's Hell," today west of Cody. Though the geysers and mud pots are gone, the river is still known as the "Stinking Water" by the Natives—and the Shoshone River by the USGS.

While Bridger had been a community of beauty courtesy of Buckle Bunny Lake, Colter was a dirty but rich railroad town. Born because it was the confluence of three railroad track systems and two overland trails that became highways, it was a way station for anyone and everyone crossing the Badlands.

What Colter lacked in scenery—it was flat as a pancake with the Laramie Mountains nothing more than a slight visual blip on the horizon— it more than made up for with the money that could be made in town. A transportation, insurance, banking, and investment center for the wealthy in the surrounding three counties, Colter was where you made money, invested money, and watched money. But you did not live in Colter for the weather, view, or creature comforts.

"We are a split community," Police Chief Virgil Fenster told Noonan. "By that I mean half of the community is well off and getting better. The other half is working class, cowboys, mechanics, service personnel, and the like. It's our roots," he said pronouncing the word *roots* as *ruts*. "In this town, *on the other side of the tracks* has a real Western meaning. The west end of town is a pill hill and banker's row. The east end, on the other side of the tracks, is where the less well-heeled live. Race, religion, and education have nothing to do with it. We've got rich Indians, Jews, Muslims, and blacks living uptown and the same mix downtown."

"I really didn't need to know that," Noonan started to say as he pulled his notebook form his battered briefcase.

"Not a problem," Fenster said as he dug through the pile of paper on his desk. "I know why you're here, so I've pulled together what I have. I also know you like to be called Heinz, Heinz, so here's what I have." He handed Noonan three sheets of paper.

"Not much for a robbery."

"Not much to say. Slick job, well planned. Like corn through a goose. Hit the two shops on the Fourth of July. Best time for the good money. While we were investigating the coin store robbery, they were taking down the jewelry store. When we got to the jewelry store, they were gone, mixing with the crowd at the Fourth of July rodeo and fair we have every year. So we got nothing but a description and a list of stolen items."

"No security cameras?"

"Nope. They had them, but they weren't turned on. Bodacious people are cheap."

This was a heart-stopper for Noonan, and his body language was a tell. "Bodacious . . ." Noonan tried to say calm. "Relatives of the Bodacious brothers in Washakie?"

"Cousins, in-laws, whatever. The Bodacious are a big family in these parts. Lots of loose pieces if you know what I mean. Great-granddad came in with the railroad in the 1870s. Got lots of land the old-fashioned way."

"Killing Indians and taking their land?"

"Some of it. Bought other lots. Homesteaded. Crafty geezer. Did very well for himself. Outlived three wives and more than a few children. It's a big family that spread out. Bridger, Colter, Washakie in this part of the Badlands. There are Bodacious families in Cheyenne, Rawlins, Lusk, Cody, Casper, Buffalo. Big family, really spread out. Got a lot of founding families that way."

"But the Bodacious brothers in Washakie were in the coin and jewelry business. The same here. A coincidence?"

"We thought so and did some digging. Yes, they are related—cousins. But the coincidence ended there. The coin and jewelry stores in Bridger are owned by two different families, neither of them related to the Bodacious in any way. Just small businesses. The take in Washakie and Bridger was small. Here it was sizeable."

"How sizeable?"

"Sixty thousand dollars wholesale. All of it insured and none of it on consignment."

"From both coin and jewelry store?"

"Yup. Both stores. The coin store was peanuts, about five thousand dollars. The big money was in the jewelry. The good news, though, the stones stolen were all Gemprint, so we might be able to get the perps at the back end."

"If you ever get the gems back."

"True. But that's neither here nor there when it comes to the robbery." Fenster pointed to the report in Noonan's hand. "As far as the robbery is concerned, you know the story. Tall man, short woman with masks robbed both stores. MO matches. Gloves, so no fingerprints. We checked trash cans between the jewelry store and the rodeo grounds . . ."

"How far was that?"

"Six, eight blocks. We found nothing. We did some searches of people coming out of the fairgrounds but got nothing. No one was happy about being searched, but we got nothing."

"I'm guessing you had so many out-of-towners that a search of the hotels and motels did no good."

"We're one step ahead of you. Yes, we were loaded with out-of-towners, but we did check all the guests from the hotels and motels, all six of them. There are ten B&Bs, and we got the names of all tall men and short women. We compared the list with Bridger because it had the robbery six weeks earlier. Then we compared the list with Washakie PD after their robbery."

"Any names cross-check?"

"About a dozen but they were bureaucrats, people who move around a lot."

"How about Darby O'Reilly?"

"Everyone's interested in O'Reilly these days. Yes, he was here. Doing the computerization stuff. He was working at the county courthouse when the robberies occurred. I double-checked because you had asked about him in Bridger."

"How far is the county courthouse from the coin and jewelry stores?"

"Mile or so. I doubt he had anything to do with the robberies. He was locked in the county courthouse."

"Why locked in?"

"Fourth of July is a holiday. Federal, state, and local. But the computerization project had a federal-funding deadline, so he had to be working on the fourth."

"Was he alone in the courthouse?"

"Yup. Just for you, we checked. Wyoming is a small . . ."

"State. Yes, I keep hearing that," Noonan said with a smile. "So you double-checked your evidence."

"Absolutely." Fenster smiled like the Cheshire cat as he paused. "Security cameras were double-checked when we knew you were going to ask about him. He went in alone, came out alone."

"Are the O'Reillys a big family hereabouts?"

"Old, yes. Large, no. Darby's grandfather came in with the state. Worked as a bureaucrat, and his son took the same job. Then Darby took the same job. One son per family. Darby's single but has a new girlfriend in Bridger. That's why he spends so much time there."

"Speaking of families, how about the Harrisons?"

"All Harrisons we know are above snakes. We checked them out right after the Washakie murder."

"Darby O'Reilly have any business dealing with the Bodacious family?"

"Darby?" Fenster laughed. "The Bodacious family everywhere is into everything that has a dime: banking, insurance, grocery stores, land speculation. They're even getting involved with the photovoltaic people over in Washakie. Darby? He's living in the same house his grandfather paid off. He's probably got a retirement with the State of Wyoming and savings. No, he's small potatoes. Bodacious are big time. No link I've heard of."

"Are the Bodacious part of the Nimerigar operation? I hear there's a casino being planned."

"A lot of people in Washakie have been smoking locoweed. The Nimerigar got fifty thousand acres of nothing. No access to the interstate. No water on the land. No access to any of the power lines. No money to advertise. Sure, I hear they've been talking to casinos, and I also hear one casino tossed some seed money. Just in case, you know. But, seriously, to make a casino profitable, it has to be big and bright and accessible to lots and lots of people. That does not fit the Nimerigar land."

"Suppose the Nimerigar could get the water and power, would a casino be reasonable?"

"Anything's possible. With water and power and land, they would have a chance to get a casino to cash in big time. But there's still the problem of access. To get to the casino the gamblers would have to drive around Robin Hood's barn. That means getting off the interstate and driving through Colter or Bridger, depending on which way they are coming, then the two hours to Washakie, and then down a fifteen-mile dirt road."

"So, the Bodacious do not have any part in the Nimerigar plans with the casino?"

"If they do, I don't know about it. But if there's a dime in it, they do. Or will. The Bodacious family, the rich ones anyway, think long term. So, yeah, I'd say they had a toe in the water. But only a toe. They're no one's fools. At least not the Bodacious family here in Colter. In Washakie, the family is strictly nickel-and-dime." The Police Chief paused. "If you really want to know about the Bodacious family, talk to Harold Bodacious. He's a lawyer here in Colter and a slippery character you've never met. He's also the lawyer for that Italian company that bought out Laramie Consolidate Syndicate."

CHAPTER 42

It was big time for Wyoming. Big time in a small state simply meant the governor showed up. In a large state, this would have been big news in the local press, but in Wyoming, everyone knew the governor, so when she showed up, it was just another day when the governor showed up. She cut ribbons all the time and issued press releases honoring a boy scout, a first responder, a visiting athlete, or a turkey farmer. This was Wyoming, and not much was a *big deal*.

So the big time consisted of the governor showing up at the Wyoming Department of Lands and offering her congratulations on the completion of the computerization of the land records. This was a long time in coming, she noted, and Wyoming was just about the last state to bring its land records into the twenty-first century. She made a joke about the office doing a "land office business" to bring the records up to date and congratulated the office—with a staff of one, Darby O'Reilly—for his diligence in shepherding the project. O'Reilly received a handshake from the governor, a Wyoming certificate of merit, and a desk weight with his name beneath the Great Seal of the State of Wyoming.

Then the governor left.

So did O'Reilly.

Now that the computerization of land records was complete, he was going to take a well-deserved vacation, he told his coworkers in the DMV office. He was going on a Caribbean cruise. He'd be back in two weeks, and he left with a curious, unusual smile on his face.

CHAPTER 43

Harold Bodacious was as slippery a lawyer as Heinz Noonan, the "Bearded Holmes," had ever met in his career. And Noonan had met many a slippery lawyer. The law office of Harold Bodacious was a coiffured attempt at passing him off as a *good old country boy*. His only receptionist was in her seventies, and his office assistant was a relative. Noonan knew that because of the nameplate on the man's desk. The office was clean and well kept, had no dust, and had a threadbare carpet on the floor and four wooden chairs in front of Harold's desk. The desk itself was of generic wood and had last been polished when Richard Nixon was president of the United States.

Harold Bodacious was pushing eighty, but he looked sixty. Fit and agile, he rose from behind the desk and shook Noonan's hand when the detective offered it. Bodacious did not wear a tie or sport a bolo. He also had a harassed look, as if he had been working hard all day, which Noonan immediately recognized as show.

"I'm glad you could see me on such short notice." Noonan said as he sat down.

"Not a problem," Bodacious responded with a smile that was wolfish. "I always have time for law and order."

157

"Coming right to the point because your time is valuable, I'd like to know if there is any link between the Stupinigi Corporation and the Nimerigar operation."

"Ah, the Nimerigar. A restless organization. When one has a large nose, he believes everyone is talking about it. Just between the two of us," Bodacious said and then indicated that Noonan should put his notebook away, "I'd be more than happy to oblige you. As long as you don't write it down. Let's just make this person-to-person."

Noonan knew what "person-to-person" meant. It meant he was going to be told a lie.

But he put his notebook away anyway.

Bodacious leaned back in his wood chair—which creaked. Noonan knew an act when he saw it, and Bodacious was living up to his image as an amiable, old country lawyer.

Noonan was not fooled. This man was going to give him a line of buffalo manure.

"There are quite a few links between the Stupinigi corporation and the Nimerigar. But it's important to keep in mind that the Stupinigi Corporation is a composite business force. In other words, if you go into their office you can see contracts, books, legal documents, annual reports. The Nimerigar are not a composite operation. Until they become a unified entity, there is no one who speaks for the entire association. What this means is what you hear in Washakie may not be what is being said in Colter or Bridger."

"Further," he continued, "the contact the Stupinigi Corporation has had with the Nimerigar is limited to people *who say* they are the Nimerigar. It has been very frustrating, from a legal point of view, because the Stupinigi Corporation has interests that coincide with Nimerigar interests."

"Like?" Noonan pressed him.

Bodacious smiled like a fox in a hen house. "It is no secret that the Nimerigar are making contacts in Las Vegas. The Stupinigi Corporation has land adjacent to the Nimerigar property. If the casino goes in, the Stupinigi Corporation will be a neighbor and benefit. But it is not a one-way street. The Stupinigi Corporation can, shall we say, enhance the effect of the casino by participating as a partner in some of its enterprise."

"Like a power-line corridor?"

"You live up to your reputation, Heinz. Yes, a power-line corridor. The Stupinigi Corporation has purchased the old Laramie Consolidate Syndicate property. Those lands will take the proposed photovoltaic power lines to within a few miles of the Wyoming transmission lines and the national power grid. But the Corporation is taking a gamble. Unless it can cut a deal, to be crude, with the Nimerigar Association, the access corridor is worthless."

"So the Stupinigi Corporation is gambling that it can cut a deal with the Nimerigar with the transmission corridor as bait."

"Not really. The deal will be with the photovoltaic company who will be on Nimerigar land. It's quite complicated. Like I said, dealing with the Nimerigar is quite difficult right now. There is no bona fide point of contact. No legal one, that is. Not yet."

"So the Nimerigar are not actively involved in negotiations with the Stupinigi Corporation."

Bodacious smiled. "I didn't say that. To answer your question, yes, the Stupinigi Corporation is dealing with the Nimerigar on a broad range of issues. After all, they share dozens of miles of property lines. They have to deal with each other. But as far as legal matters, until the Nimerigar form a legal corporation, have a board of directors with the authority to sign on behalf of all the members, no, there are no legal documents between the two."

"But there will be?"

"Soon. The Stupinigi Corporation will not make a dime off its investment unless the photovoltaic plant comes on line. And the photovoltaic company will not make a dime until the casino is a reality."

"How about water?"

"Water is yet another problem. Both are possible for the Nimerigar land, but it will take a lot of wheeling and dealing. The Nimerigar and Stupinigi Corporation need transportation corridors to be successful. Title-free corridors, let me add. The roadway is a given since the Stupinigi Corporation owns the land from Cannibal Pass to the interstate."

Noonan cut in, "But the land for the power line and waterline are a problem."

"Right now, yes. But such problems can be worked out."

Then Noonan pulled a fast one. "I'm told a lot of land that the corridors will cross are owned by the Bodacious family."

"You are well informed. Yes. But you clearly do not come from a large family. You can pick your friends, but you cannot pick your family. The Bodacious is a large, old, and shall we say, diverse collection of individuals, many of whom avoid family gatherings."

"Like the Bodacious brothers in Washakie who got robbed?"

"As I said, you are well informed. Harry and Sam are part of the Bodacious family, but they are not welcome by the extended family in any community except Washakie. In Washakie they have immediate family, which, shall we say, has no choice but to embrace the siblings. For the rest of us, Jimmy Carter had Billy, Barak Obama has Malik, and Ivanka has Donald. It's a sad reality of life."

Noonan smelled an angle. "So the Bodacious family, in pieces, parts, or as whole is not dealing with the Stupinigi Corporation or the Nimerigar over land issues?"

"There's a lot of talk. But then again, this is Wyoming, and land is money. No one has signed anything, if that's what you mean. Like I said before, there is no one with legal authority within the Nimerigar operation to sign for the company. So nothing is going to happen until there is a single point of contact."

"When will that happen?"

"Today, tomorrow, next week. Legally, it could happen within an hour. Joshua Three Trees has proxies from enough Nimerigar to form a corporation. A temporary board of directors could be chosen and a president elected. Then it would simply be a matter of signing some papers and getting a notary stamp."

A bell went off in the deep recess of Noonan's mind. "So once that paperwork is signed, the Stupinigi Corporation and the Nimerigar can do business."

"Yes, Heinz. And I know you like to be called Heinz. Wyoming is a small state."

"I keep hearing that."

"Heinz, once the Nimerigar have a single point of contact, yes the Stupinigi will do business with them. But you are jumping a massive chasm by assuming that once the deal is inked, the casino can move forward. The combined lands of the Stupinigi Corporation and the Nimerigar will still not include corridors to the power grid or the waters of Buckle Bunny Lake. Those corridors must be negotiated with private landowners. That could take some time."

"Rome wasn't built in a day."

"Wyoming is not Rome, but you've got it right."

CHAPTER 44

Wyoming was a land of firsts. It was the first state to have a county public library. The first book printed in Wyoming was a dictionary of the Sioux language. It had the nation's first National Park, Yellowstone, and the first dude ranch, the term "dude" being coined in Wyoming. It was the first state to allow women to vote, and, in 1925, Mrs. Nellie Tayloe Ross—Tayloe being spelled correctly—became the first female governor in the country. Wyoming also had its oddities. Residents of Cheyenne cannot take showers on Wednesday; you cannot use a firearm to fish; Wyoming residents overweight by one hundred pounds or more cannot use park equipment; and, in Newcastle, it is illegal for couples to have sex while standing up in a store's walk-in freezer.

Humor aside, Wyoming also has a dark side to its history. It is rooted in the ancient expression repeated many times throughout history, paraphrased as "it may be illegal, but what are you going to do about it?"

Wyoming had a sordid history of the big pushing out the small.

The roots of modern Wyoming were sunk into the Badlands in 1866 when a rancher named Nelson Story, Sr. drove one thousand cattle to Montana through Wyoming. He recognized the potential of Wyoming as cattle country, and the word spread quickly. By 1873 the Wyoming Stock

Growers Association was formed, and it rapidly became both the power behind the throne and the throne itself of territorial government. It was the classic story of the rich and powerful driving out the small. Claiming that the small ranchers were involved in rustling, the Wyoming Stock Growers Association hired "regulators"—translated into street language as "hired killers"—to clear up the matter. Thus were men like Frank M. Canton hired. Canton was one of the worst. To quote Western historian Harry Sinclair Drago, Canton was a "merciless, congenital, emotionless killer. For pay, he murdered eight—very likely ten—men."

What erupted became known as the Johnson County War or the War on the Powder River. In either case it resulted in bloody confrontations. It did not take long for the small ranchers to understand that unless they stood together, they would all die separately. So they organized a posse of over two hundred men to fight the regulators. The war only ended when President Benjamin Harrison sent the US Cavalry to Wyoming to restore law and order.

A century and a half later, the same forces that had erupted during the Johnson County War were still present. But this time the war was not over cattle. It was over water. Mark Twain famously said, "Whiskey is for drinking—water is for fighting over." He might have said it of California, but it rang true in Wyoming.

It was all about water. Land with no water was cheap. Land with access to water was precious. Noonan knew that *precious* meant *expensive*, and *expensive* meant he might have found his big-money link to the murder and three robberies. They had to be pieces of the same jigsaw puzzle. But if they were—and he believed them to be—there was a time element involved. The murder and the robberies happened when they did for a reason that had something to do with time. There was a clock ticking somewhere. Time was running out for the "Bearded Holmes." He knew it, but, at that moment, all he knew for certain was that he had a tabletop of loose pieces of the same puzzle, and none of them seemed to fit.

163

CHAPTER 45

It is generally conceded by historians of Western Civilization that our cultural roots began with the seeds sown by the Egyptian empire—in spite of the fact that Egypt, ancient or modern, is in the East, not West. That irony aside, historian credit the initial inklings of civilization with the formation of the First Dynasty by the first pharaoh, Menes, who unified Upper and Lower Egypt under a single ruler. From that moment, about three thousand years before the Christian era to Roger Bacon in 1215, the loudest noise any human heard was thunder. Bacon was the first to record the explosion of gunpowder.

In the West.

In the East, the Chinese had been using gunpowder since the year 142 when it was discovered that mixing the three critical powders would cause particles to "fly and dance" about violently and produce a loud noise. Western inventors used gunpowder for guns—the Chinese, for fireworks.

In the case of either civilization, West and East, until the dawn of gunpowder, the loudest man-made nose was that of bells. In the early days, bells were the exclusive province of religion, and their ringing served as a clock for those with no watches, a good thing since the first known timepiece dates from the 1530s. Thus did religious time become merchant time. The ringing of church bells at noon, it should be added, is not because it is noon. Rather, it is a practice that began in July 1456. Beginning on July 4, Ottoman Sultan Mehmed II had the city of Belgrade under siege. Constantinople had fallen to the Turks three years earlier, and the Ottoman Empire was on the advance. There was very little Christian Europe could do to help the besieged city of Belgrade except pray. So Pope Callixtus III went one better. He ordered that all bells in Christendom be rung at noon every day to remind the faithful to pray for the Christian defenders against the Ottomans who were Muslims. Before the order could be transmitted to all the churches in Europe, the defenders of Belgrade pulled a surprise counterattack and swamped the Ottoman forces, forcing them to retreat. When word of the victory reached Europe, the ringing of the bell at noon for prayer was transformed into a commemoration of victory of the Christians over the Ottomans. Callixtus III never canceled the order of ringing bells at noon and, to this day, Christian church bells ring at noon around the world.

Just as important, church bells also served as a warning of danger. As early as the days of William the Conqueror—who died in 1087, about the same year most grandparents were born—bells were used as nightly curfew. They chimed in London at 8:00 p.m. as the gates of the city were about to be closed. If you could not make it into the city by that hour, you could spend a dangerous night among the bandits who prowled outside the city gate. Three hundred years later, Marco Polo wrote of a curfew in what is now known as Beijing, then called Peking. After the third stroke of a "great bell suspended in a lofty building," guards in bands of thirty or forty would prowl the streets looking for miscreants. In Europe, some cities were convinced that the bells at night frightened wolves. Rinchnach in Bavaria, a city of barely three thousand, continues this practice of frightening wolves to this day. How many wolves have been frightened from the city since the days of the Black Plague is not recorded.

In America, the bell became associated with fire. In colonial times, a night watchman would alert the citizens to a fire with the ringing of a bell. The practice was carried forward when there were fire stations. A bell would alert the fireman that his assistance was needed. It was said that the ringing of the fire bell left such a strong impression that horses that had been retired from fire-department duty continued to run to fires long after they had been sold for dray animals whenever they heard a fire bell. So powerful was the image of the bell in American history that Thomas Jefferson famously compared slavery in the United States as a "fire bell in the night." He was correct. Slavery did generate a conflagration that swept the nation two generations after his death.

Well into the twenty-first century, bells were still both a reminder of our heritage and a metaphor. In addition to the fire bell, used equally frequently with fire alarm, a memory, often negative, is said to "ring a bell." Today, when something "rings a bell" it is a portend of an impending matter that one had experienced before. One must always be aware of the tolling of a bell because, to plagiarize both John Donne and Ernest Hemingway, "it is tolling for thee."

Heinz Noonan, chief of detectives of the Sandersonville Police Department, was well aware of the tolling of a bell no matter how distant or faint. No matter how soft and indiscriminate the peal, he heard it. Even more important, he took it as an exhortation. In his experience, when he heard the bell, he took it as a hint that something of merit had just occurred. Of specifically what he would not know at the time. But he knew whatever it was, it was important. Once the distant toll of a bell—most often in the singular—was sensed, he knew the spear point of something important had just touched the hull of his ship of inquiry.

In the office of Harold Bodacious, he had picked up the distant toll of a bell.

It was time for a change of direction, the moment to reorient his thinking. Besides the murder, the great unanswered question in this matter was simply "Where was the money?" Every great crime occurs for a great amount of money. Someone, or several someones, had been going through a great deal of trouble to muddy the investigative waters. Noonan was sure the three robberies were connected to the murder, but he could not see a clear link. But he could see several links between the robberies. Two of the three robberies were witnessed by members of the Bodacious clan. This could be a coincidence, but Noonan was loathe to give coincidence its due—even when it was deserved. Second, there was a link between a witness, Sandra Trucco, and someone, Darby O'Reilly, who had been in all three towns when the robberies occurred. Third, the Nimerigar had just received fifty thousand acres of land, which could be a financial windfall if they could coordinate the acquisition of water, power, and access. All three required some action on land, which linked them with Darby O'Reilly and thus with Sandra Trucco.

Then there was the sudden appearance of the Stupinigi Corporation. Noonan was sure that the intent of the company was to take advantage of the proposed casino. After all, if the casino went in—against all odds—the value of the Stupinigi property would increase.

Maybe.

That was the big question. If a casino went in, the Stupinigi land would still be rattlesnake country. What would make the Nimerigar property increase in value was the use of the land. But there was no reasonable use of the Stupinigi land other than a roadway across it from the interstate to the Nimerigar land. How could the Stupinigi Corporation make money on a road that already legally crossed its land?

But there was still big money in the mix. Where it was, Heinz Noonan was not sure. Yet. He was not sure yet. But he could not see how there *was not* money in the mix. The murder, three robberies, and the Nimerigar land were all connected. But, at this moment, he could not see the connection.

It was all very convoluted, but then again, solving crimes with big money were never easy.

Had this been a usual crime, Noonan would have gone back to the proverbial Square One and looked to see if there was anything he had missed. But there was no Square One here. The only forensic at the murder scene was blood and DNA. The three robberies were ancient history at this point in time, and Harrison Day Three was unresponsive. He did not have a lot of solid options.

So he used a side door.

He played a hunch. The one player, or nonplayer, in the mix was the federal government. Thus he played the only card he had. The next morning he headed for the one place he knew he could find the most knowledgeable federal people in Wyoming.

167

He made the hour-and-a-half trip to Cheyenne in three hours, thanks to highway construction and then had to wait an hour for the BLM land office egress officer to get back from lunch.

"Heinz, isn't it?" the man said when he came back from the diner still munching a sandwich.

"I'm getting to be well known in these parts."

"We're a small state," the egress officer said, lifting his pop in salute. "Everyone knows everything."

"Tough place to have a secret." Noonan smiled.

"If you want to keep a secret in Wyoming," the egress officer said as he smiled, "live in Utah."

"Well, if Wyoming is so small, you probably know why I'm here."

"I know why you're here," the egress officer said still smiling. "But I'm not sure my answers will satisfy you."

"Humor me."

"Not a problem. The murder and robberies are way out of our jurisdiction. So, my best guess, you want to know if there is a way for the Nimerigar to do anything with their land."

"You guess good." Noonan said smiling. "And the answer is . . ." he let the sentence hang.

"Well, how much to you know about land?"

"If you want to live somewhere, you have to have it."

The egress officer laughed. "OK. Good answer. Let me come at your problem from a different angle. Let me tell you what you can't do."

"Any way I get my answer is fine."

"I'm going to treat you as if you are a member of the general public who doesn't know anything about land ownership, egress, roads, corridors."

Noonan pointed to his face. "Note the look of surprise on my face."

The egress officer smiled. "I'm going to use that expression with my mother-in-law. Let's start with basics. The Nimerigar have fifty thousand acres, which is about twenty miles by fifteen miles. If you don't live in Wyoming, that seems like a lot of land. But the value of land in Wyoming depends on three things: access, water, and power. You can have a lot of land, but if you can't get to the land because it's on the side of a mountain, for instance, it has no value. You can't live on the land without water, and if you want to do any kind of business—like mining or a casino—you've got to have power. To have power you need a road to bring in fuel, like diesel, or be able to link into the Wyoming power grid. The closest the Nimerigar land comes to the power grid is about fifteen miles."

Noonan started to say something, but the egress officer waved him off.

"Now that fifty thousand acres have problems. This is Wyoming, and nothing is simple here. First off, that fifty thousand is not in a big square. Even way out in the Badlands, a lot of people own property in the area. There were homesteads, mining claims, easements, rights, and frontier roads. So the fifty thousand acres has a border that snakes around existing land claims. Then there are access routes to lands and mines that people may or may not be using now but could in the future. You can't close off those roadways even if no one has used them in a century, and some of those roadways run through the Nimerigar acreage. Then there are critical habitat acreages and historical structures, which may or may not be out there, and archaeological sites, which may or may not be out there—all of which require special county, state, and federal permits to build on, much less cross. Then there are dump sites, some with very hazardous waste that need to be cleaned up before construction can begin, graves—white and Indian—along with crime scenes from cold cases, which may or may not be discovered today, tomorrow or a year from now. Sure, the Nimerigar got fifty thousand acres, but getting to use those acres is not a slam dunk."

Noonan shook his head as if to clear it. "So, it's not as simple as just extending a pipeline to Buckle Bunny Lake and stringing wires to the Wyoming power grid."

The egress officer laughed. "You're thinking logically, and land ownership is not logical, rational, reasonable, or planned. We are talking one hundred and fifty years of people staking land and making claims—some of which are extinct, and others which are still active—on paper. This is not a simple matter. Since we are playing a mind game here, let's get the most obvious possibilities out of the way. Remember, we're just playing mind games here. Real-life land issues are a lot more convoluted."

"I'll take what I can get," Noonan said smiling. "And keep the words short and simple so someone like me can understand what you are talking about."

The egress officer laughed. "I'll try. Land issues get very complicated very fast. So, let's pretend it was the good old days. That was before 1976. Prior to 1976 you could homestead in a lot of areas in Wyoming. What that meant was that you could claim 160 acres of land as yours if you improved it and lived on it for five years. If the Nimerigar had received their land in the good old days, they could have gotten three or four members of the organization to homestead land in long rectangles that stretched from the fifty thousand acres they have all the way to Buckle Bunny Lake. There are 43,560 square feet per acre so one hundred and sixty acres has about seven million square feet. If your homestead was, say, one hundred yards wide, just enough to accommodate a water pipeline, a road, and a transmission corridor, you could include about thirteen running miles of homestead. Four l-o-n-g homesteads could have reached Buckle Bunny Lake—that is, as long as the land was being worked and someone was living on it for five years."

"But that all changed in 1976?"

"Right. In 1976 Congress passed what is known as the BLM Organic Act, which ended homesteading. After 1976, we, the BLM, that is, could sell federal land at market value. True, badlands are not very valuable because they are, well, badlands. But by 1976 people had been homesteading in Wyoming for almost a century. Then Wyoming became a state in 1890, and the State of Wyoming had a hand in land sales and status. Then . . ."

"Did statehood make it simpler?"

"Not a chance. See, you are thinking about land as someplace where you grow crops and build a cabin or a sod hut. People have been playing fast and loose with land status for a century and half. Mining operations claimed land and then made roads across the badlands to their claims. No one told them *no*, so they just did it. Then homesteaders used the roads. Some of those roads are still in use; others are abandoned."

"By abandoned, do you mean the ownership went back to the federal government?"

"That's another yes and no. Mining companies bought each other out. So the Smith Mine in 1870 might have been sold to the Jones Company in 1890. Then the Jones Company was bought by the Harris Company who combined with the Whitford Company that was bought out by the Union Pacific. The original mining claim is thus active in the sense that someone owns it, which means the road is still active."

"But if any one of those companies went bankrupt then the land and roadway went back to the federal government?"

"Not really. A lot of so-called federal land became state land in 1890 when Wyoming became a state. And some state land became county land. It's not simple."

"But the roads could be used for pipelines and transmission lines?"

"Not an easy question to answer. Most of the roads you are talking about, no. An access road, or what we call an egress road"—he waved his hand in the air of his office—"has a specific definition. It can only be used for a road, and that road cannot be any wider than its original use. So, no, you cannot take a two-rut road and turn it into a football-field-wide road and run a water pipeline from Buckle Bunny Lake."

"How could you get a pipeline from Buckle Bunny Lake to the Nimerigar land?"

"An easy question with a complicated answer. Water pipelines are expensive, so they have to be built in a straight line. Well, sort of. Wyoming does have earthquakes, so the water pipeline is not going to be solid and straight as an arrow. So, to have the water pipeline make an almost beeline to Nimerigar land, about fifty miles, it would have to cross a lot of private land. Every foot of that private land would need an easement of some kind, but that would be very hard to do."

"Why?"

"An easement means reasonable access. You can't build a road to your property through someone else's cornfield. That's not reasonable. So you'd have to claim the right to an access road across land that's vacant even though it's owned by someone. This makes it sound very simple but it's not. Now multiply the problems a pipeline would face by the number of owners of land between Buckle Bunny Lake and Nimerigar land, and you can see there are real problems."

"How much state and federal land is there between Buckle Bunny Lake and Nimerigar land?"

"A lot. But it's in swatches. Access across state and federal lands is almost a guarantee unless there is critical game habitat or some historically significant acres. We wouldn't know that until the plans for the pipeline are presented. But most businesses can work around the restrictions. It's expensive but not hard. The big problem with any pipeline is crossing private land. The Nimerigar are private citizens, so the right of eminent domain cannot be used."

"You mean a court cannot order the private landowner to give up part of his land for the pipeline."

"Basically, yes. It's more complicated, but, as you said, to keep it simple, yes."

"OK, how about power lines?"

"Same basic problem as with the waterline. The only real difference is that the power lines can snake their way across the badlands."

"Then there's the access road to Nimerigar land. That's being used now. Can it be expanded for more traffic?"

"Not unless the landowner, in this case the Stupinigi Corporation, sells them the land. Without a transfer of land, the road is as wide as it can be as an access road. The only way it can be expanded is to buy the land on both sides of the road and then do the expansion."

"How about flying people onto the land? If they cannot arrive by access road, can gamblers be flown in?"

The egress officer laughed. "More of that Nimerigar pipe dream. Sure, you could fly in gamblers. There's enough space on Nimerigar land to have an airport. But don't forget, running an airport will require water and power. Then there's the problem of fuel for the planes. It's not reasonable to fly it in. It has to come over the road, and that road is not built for fuel trucks. Keep in mind the only road into Nimerigar land, from either direction, is basically two ruts. Even if you put down asphalt, it's still one car wide."

"So a casino is not possible?"

"I didn't say that. The idea was bandied about long before the Nimerigar got their fifty thousand acres. There are a lot of gamblers who don't want to fly to Las Vegas or Atlantic City. They want to drive. Right now Wyoming only allows gambling on horse and dog races—and charitable Bingo games and the like, which is why most people believe the Nimerigar wanted their land. It's Indian land, and a casino on Indian land anywhere in the United States is legal. The Nimerigar have been wheeling and dealing with a New York photovoltaic company that would solve the power problem. At least initially."

Noonan was taken by surprise. "Why only initially?"

"Economies of scale. The smallest photovoltaic operation, if that's what they are called, will produce more power than the casino can use. So what are they going to do with the excess power? The traditional answer is to wheel it—that is, put it into the power-line grid. Then extra power in Wyoming, say, could be wheeled into Colorado where the population is larger. But you cannot wheel power if you cannot connect to the electrical power grid."

"Why not use the water pipeline corridor?"

"You could if *there was* a water pipeline corridor. The same with the road. If the roadway was wider, you might be able to run the power lines down the right-of-way."

"But the road is as wide as it is going to get."

"You said it. I didn't."

"So the chances of a casino are pretty slim."

The egress officer smiled. "This is Wyoming, and anything is possible. The key to the success of a casino is a land corridor giving the land access to water coming in and power going out. But to have that access, you need to have land ownership or egress rights of the corridor acreage. As far as we,"—again he waved his hand around the office—"are concerned, we'll sell the corridor acreage on federal lands at market rate, which is very low. And the State of Wyoming will do the same for state land. But that won't get you squat unless you have bought out the corridor acreage across the private land. And when it comes to Buckle Bunny Lake, the nearest reasonable supply of water, the land around the lake and back about five miles was claimed and improved long ago."

"Same for the road?"

"Same for the road," the egress officer agreed. "The only difference is that the land for the road is owned by one entity, the Stupinigi Corporation. Then it's just a matter of price. But that only gives you the road, not the water or the power corridors."

"Where's the State of Wyoming in all of this?"

"As far as the State of Wyoming is concerned, you're a day late and a dollar short. The man you'd want to talk to is Darby O'Reilly. He's the land man for the State of Wyoming. He just finished computerizing the entire land picture of private and state land in Wyoming so it would mesh with our lands, the federal lands. Now you can just pull up land status of any square foot of private, country, or state land and see who owns it."

"Why am I day late?"

"The ceremony for the completion of the computerization was yesterday. O'Reilly got a certificate of merit and left for vacation. You'll have to wait for him to get back."

And, again, that distant bell in the deep recesses of Noonan's cerebral cortex clanged. This time a bit louder.

"Tell me about buying land," Noonan said with a smile.

The egress officer smiled back. "Thinking of buying a few acres? Got lots of wolf-spider habitat available."

"Is it on the ocean?"

The egress officer laughed. "Give global warming a thousand years, and, yeah, it'll be on the coastline." Then he got serious. "Generally speaking, and keeping it as simple as possible, there are there kinds of land in this area: federal, state, and private. We are the custodian of the federal lands. Again, keeping it simple, there are two types of federal lands: land you can buy and land you cannot buy. You cannot buy national-park land, for instance, or critical habitat. Other types of land, you can buy. It's called over-the-counter land, and you just come in and put in an order for land. If we can sell it, we sell it at market value."

"What's the market value of badlands land?" Noonan asked.

"Pretty cheap. People and companies do not buy land to use. At least not right away. It's bought for long-term possibilities."

"How many people have been buying land from BLM in the Washakie area lately?"

The BLM egress man smiled. "Getting in on the casino craze, are you?"

"So there has been an uptick in land sales in the Washakie area?"

"Depends on what you mean by area. Near Washakie, yes, but just one company: Stupinigi Corporation. But it has been a pastiche of properties.

Yes, near Washakie but a lot of other areas as well. About three years ago, the Stupinigi Corporation bought out an East Coast investment conglomerate that owned large chunks of land in the Washakie area."

"Anywhere near the Nimerigar land?"

"Bordering it, as a matter of fact. About the same time. But there's not a link, if that's what you are implying. Actually, there is, but it is a negative one."

"How's that?"

"As the Nimerigar land was being selected"—the egress man stalled for a moment—"*selected* means you are choosing the land you want to buy, and then you do a title search to see if someone else owns it. Just because it's in the middle of nowhere does not mean no one ones it. Anyway, as the Nimerigar were selecting their land, Stupinigi bought out the East Coast conglomerate of all its Wyoming land. It was worth next to nothing, so the conglomerate was willing to sell."

"But with a casino going in, the land could be worth a lot more," Noonan said.

"Not really. The casino is years away, and the East Coast conglomerate has been holding onto the acreage for a century. It was land that had been through a number of corporations before the First World War and then went belly-up. It was originally part of the Laramie Consolidate Syndicate that was a gold mine in the 1890s. When the mine went dry, the Syndicate just walked away. It didn't pay taxes, and the land went to the State of Wyoming."

"Why the State of Wyoming?" Noonan asked. "It was originally federal land, wasn't it?"

"Yup," the egress officer said. "Once federal land is sold, it does not come back to the feds. The Syndicate bought the land, and when the company went bust, it didn't pay its land tax, and the State of Wyoming foreclosed."

"So Stupinigi bought the land from the State of Wyoming?"

The egress officer just laughed. "Nothing is simple in land in Wyoming. No, the Stupinigi Corporation did not buy the land. Some other company a long ago bought. For a song. Then that company went bankrupt and was bought by another company that went belly-up to company after company until the Second World War when the mine reopened. The war ended, and the company went under. And another corporation bought the mine and land for a song."

"How many times did the land get bought before the Stupinigi Corporation bought it?"

"Many. How many, I don't know, but you can go over to the State of Wyoming land office and ask. Like I said before, if you had asked yesterday the main man would have been there, Darby O'Reilly, but he's on vacation."

"So the land went through a number of owners before the Stupinigi Corporation ended up with it. That was three years ago?"

"Give or take. We"—he raised the index finger of his left hand—"got involved when the Nimerigar land was conveyed, er, given to the Indians. The second—and I do mean the second—the Nimerigar land was transferred, Old Man Three Trees who was the face of the Nimerigar at the time, rolled a bulldozer from Indian land over Cannibal Pass to the interstate and into Washakie. A lot of people complained to us, but there was nothing we could do. The roadway was access and has been access for a century. Old Man Three Trees knew what he was doing."

"Was the Stupinigi corporation upset?"

"Yeah. It had just bought the land from that East Coast group. It was the first time we had heard of them. They've got a lot of land out there, all badlands. They got access themselves: the old Laramie Consolidated land; at the very least the old railroad bed runs all the way to the outskirts of Colter. A lotta land that's not worth much."

"Does the land the Stupinigi Corporation bought extend into Colter?"

"No. All the land around Colter was taken long ago. It intersects with the rural highway about ten miles out of town. It used to be a railroad corridor, so it goes all the way to where the mainline railroad still is. But all the tracks are gone. It's just open land."

"Any water there?"

"Not a drop."

"Power lines?"

"Local ones. Low power to someone who doesn't know power."

"How far is the intersection of the Stupinigi land to the Wyoming power grid?"

"What you mean is, could the Stupinigi land be used for a transmission line from the Nimerigar land to the high-transmission wires."

"You read me like a book."

"A few miles but the intervening land is all private."

'You guys are way ahead of me."

"No," the egress officer said. "It's just that we've seen all kinds of schemes and scams."

"I'm sure you have," Noonan responded as he looked at his notebook. "You said that a lot companies acquired what became the Stupinigi land over the years. Where could I get a list?"

"State Archives. They're open. You probably drove past them on your way here. Ask them for their corporate index. The active corporations are online. The older ones are on microfilm."

Again, and louder, the bell.

The State of Wyoming Historical Archives and Records Center was easy to find, and the staff was ecstatic to see Noonan.

"You're here!"

"You know who I am?" Noonan was surprised.

"Wyoming is a small state," the desk clerk said. "Besides, we got a call from BLM. We already have your package ready for you."

Talk of efficiency! It was exactly what Noonan had wanted. Except he didn't know what he wanted. What he got was three lists with URL links.

The historical archivist was used to dealing with people who did not know what they wanted. That's why there were historical archivists. "What you have here are three categories of corporations and links to their corporate papers—if they have corporate papers."

"What kind of company does not have corporate papers?" Noonan asked.

"Oh, you know, a company that was established in 1921 in New York that went bankrupt in 1929. The corporate papers might be in New York. Or not. In any case, all we know is that we do not have the corporate papers here. Or they do not exist at all."

"OK, so this is a list of corporations with no papers." Noonan tapped one list.

"History," the clerk told him. "We call it *history*. All we have on these corporations is a name." She pointed to the list in Noonan's hand. Then she handed him another, longer list. "These are corporations which are defunct, er, no longer in operation but do have papers. And this last list, actually just a web address, is our online page for all corporations that are active today."

Noonan combined all three lists—actually two collections of lists and one sheet of paper with a URL—and shook them. "Fine. Now, how can I match up which corporation owned which properties?"

"Well"—the desk clerk smiled—"today is your lucky day. Yesterday the State of Wyoming put all its land records online. All you have to do is pull up the ownership index by name and then type in the corporation. If there is a record of land ownership by that corporation, you will get a location."

"Even if the company has been out of business for a century?"

"If there was a land record, it will be online."

"Even a century ago?"

"If there was a piece of paper available to the State of Wyoming, it will be online.

And the bell was now audible.

CHAPTER 46

When all were present and accounted for, they locked themselves in the Julian ballroom of the Tom Horn Hotel, across town from the State of Wyoming Historical Archives and Records Center. Everyone had a laptop. Some hooked onto the Wi-Fi of the hotel. Others connected via their cell phones. Some had suitcases for greenbacks. They would need those suitcases when they went to a local bank. There was no cash here, just electronics—which were as good as cash.

Thus began the pirouette of signatures, cash, title, and electronic transfer. Everyone had something to convey and something to receive. It was a gathering where, contrary to the old saying, it was better to receive than give. In an hour it was over, and the dozen scattered with the wind. The only thing they had to do as they left Cheyenne was drive the long way around downtown to avoid the remote possibility they would see Heinz Noonan, the "Bearded Holmes," as he was visiting the offices of the BLM office or the State of Wyoming Historical Archives.

CHAPTER 47

A lot further west than Noonan was willing to go on an historical side trip was an iconic Wyoming fixture: Devils Tower. Made nationally recognizable by the movie *Close Encounters of the Third Kind*, it was an 867-foot, igneous rock butte rising abruptly from the northwestern flatlands of the state. It attracts rock-climbers from around the world and is firmly lodged in the history—and Wyoming weird—of the state. It was discovered—that is, it was first put on the map by whites—after an 1875 expedition *discovered* it.

As so often happens, something acquires a name by accident. American history is replete with such examples. Nome, Alaska, was named for a cartographic mistake by the British Navy and Buffalo, New York, is not named for the animal but the "beautiful river" on which it sits. In the case of Buffalo, the French term *beau fleuve* was later corrupted to *buffalo*. Wyoming was not immune from this trend of misnaming locations. In the case of Devils Tower, the white explorer, Colonel Richard Irving Dodge, who *discovered* the geological anomaly asked what the Indians called it. His interpreter misinterpreted the local name and told Dodge it was "Bad God's Tower." Since there was only one "bad god" in the Christian religion, "Bad God's Tower" became Devil's Tower. (It later lost its apostrophe.)

In reality, the local name of the mountain was *Bear's Lair, Bear's Den*, or *Bear's Tipi, Bear*, in this case, being a "bad god." Local legend has it that some young girls were being chased by bears, and they—the girls, not the bears—fell onto the ground and prayed to the Great Spirit for protection. The Great Spirit took pity on them and caused the ground on which they were praying to suddenly erupt upward to 867 feet. The bears, angry at the loss of an easy meal, attempted to climb the pillar, and their claws left the vertical scratches for which the tower is known. It was declared a National Monument by President Theodore Roosevelt in 1906.

Just as the Devils Tower erupted out of nowhere, so did Heinz Noonan's case. His last few days had been a pleasant interlude between murder and robberies. He had visited a part of America he had never expected to see, scouted for a ghost ship, seen human-hide shoes, marveled at a crystal-clear lake hidden in the wind-swept badlands, and now, alas, it was back to the old grind of murder, robbery, and other crimes yet to be uncovered. It had almost been a vacation.

Almost.

He was barely through the door to the Washakie Police Department when he was confronted by a thirty-something man dressed like a New York banker. Behind him was a woman who pulsated cop.

This was not a good sign.

He was correct.

"Captain Heinz Noonan?" The man had the accent of someone from the East Coast with sixteen generations of WASP, a White Anglo-Saxon Protestant. "I'm Jerome McKinley Harrison III."

"Pleased to meet you. And you are . . ." He let the sentence hang.

"I'm the son of Jerome McKinley Harrison II. I believe you have him incarcerated here."

"I don't have anyone incarcerated here. There is a man who claims to be a Harrison, and he is a person of interest in a murder. But he is not in jail. Is this the man you are speaking of?"

"Don't end your sentence with a preposition." Harrison III was imperial in his statement. "Yes, that's my father. Where is he, and when will he be released?"

If Noonan took offense at the statement concerning the preposition, he gave no indication. He simply looked beyond Harrison III at the woman who was reaching under her breast lapel. She came out with a badge.

"Special Agent Jennifer Cornwallis from the Philadelphia FBI. We have an ongoing interest in Jerome McKinley Harrison II."

"A lot of people have an interest in Mr. Harrison II." Noonan looked directly at Agent Cornwallis. "May I ask why, and how you discovered he was here?"

"Fingerprints. The Washakie Police took your Mr. Harrison's fingerprints. They popped up in our computer system."

"Your computer system? That should have happened within hours, but here you are, at least a week and a half out from the murder here in Washakie."

"True." Cornwallis was a bit perturbed. "You see, Mr. Harrison has been very clever over the years. The only time he was fingerprinted was when he volunteered for the Marines during the Vietnam era. His fingerprints IDed him as a vet, and the name Harrison is more common than you would imagine. It took a week for the name Harrison on the fingerprints to mesh with the Harrison we were searching for"—she stalled for a moment and then revised what she was going to say—"a week for us to link the Harrison fingerprints with the Harrison for whom we were looking."

"Where'd you get the fingerprints from your Mr. Harrison if he was never fingerprinted other than the time he was in the military?"

"His fingerprints matched with a social-security number. We were a low priority, and it took a while for his prints to land on the right desk."

Noonan smelled a rat. "If he is such a low priority, why are you here in Washakie?"

Cornwallis was clearly not interested in answering. Finally, reluctantly, she took a stab at the obtuse. "Mr. Harrison III, let me quickly add, is linked to some matters of national concern."

Noonan had been here before. "Bunk. What you mean is someone in Homeland Security asked your supervisor's superior's supervisor to have you fly all the way out here to the middle of nowhere to check on a vague lead that might lead to a bigger story he is going to call his own in Philadelphia."

"She, as a matter of fact," Cornwallis said rolling her eyes. "You know the lay of the land."

"OK. We've solved the politics. Now let's get down the crime. We have two Mr. Harrisons in this case. One is presumably dead. The other is possibly your father." Noonan inclined his head toward Harrison III. "The situation is not as simple as one body, one suspect, one case."

Cornwallis shook her head. "You've got no solid link between the two Harrisons?"

"We assume there is one, but we do not know for certain. The case is still young. What can you tell me about your Harrison that will help me?"

This time Cornwallis responded confidently. "That our Mr. Harrison is involved in something devious is not surprising. Harrison is a consummate but slippery lawyer. He is very careful. Before he vanished . . ."

"Disappeared," snapped Harrison III as he cut in. "He has not been convicted of any crime. That's why a missing-person report was filed."

If Cornwallis was perturbed, she didn't show it. But then again, she was an FBI agent.

"I still don't see a solid connection between your Mr. Harrison," Noonan said again pointing from Harrison II to Cornwallis, "and Harrison Day Three here. That's how we refer to him. I'm glad you've told me the fingerprints for Harrison Day Three do match a Vietnam vet by the name of Harrison, but it's thin. How do you know the vet Harrison is your father?"

"We don't," cut in Cornwallis. "That's why we're here."

Noonan shook his head slowly. "I'll tell you exactly what the Washakie Chief of Police probably told you—and the reason you're talking to me instead of him. This is an open homicide case, and it is closed to anyone without a need to know. Just being from the FBI is not a *need to know*." He emphasized the words *need to know*. "Even if it is the same man," Noonan said looking at Harrison III, "I can't tell you where he is without his permission. He has rights, and if he wanted to disappear, and there is no warrant out for him . . ." Noonan looked at Cornwallis who shook her head. ". . . All I can do is tell him someone named Jerome McKinley Harrison III is looking for him."

Then Noonan looked at Cornwallis. "That leaves you. You want me to believe that you came all the way from Philadelphia to check out a man you want to depose? That's garbage. I know the FBI. If there is someone in Dallas to be deposed, the Dallas office makes the connection. But here you are. Why are you really here in Washakie?"

There was a long moment of silence. Finally, Cornwallis gave a measured response. "Well, there are other matters."

"Don't give me that, Agent Cornwallis. It has to be something pretty big to send a Philadelphia FBI agent this far west. So, spill the beans."

Again, a long moment a silence followed by a measured response. "I can't give that many details, but it involves national security. He was involved with some Russian nationals . . ." And she let the sentence hang.

"Not good enough," snapped Noonan. "It involves the Department of Homeland Security which could not find chopsticks in a Chinese restaurant. Let me guess. Harrison III represented people including some Russians who may have laundered money. So the Department of Homeland Security leaned on the FBI to investigate. The Russians got the tip and left Pennsylvania. Harrison III had the money, and to keep his client's money from getting grabbed by the feds, he had to put it somewhere safe. Now the Department of Homeland Security wants the FBI to talk to Mr. Harrison to find out where the money is. But there's no crime here. It's not even missing money. Mr. Harrison is doing what a responsible lawyer would do: keeping his client's legal money from the rapacious hands of the Department of Homeland Security. Once money gets taken by the department, it could sit for years. As long as Harrison stays gone, his client's money is safe." Noonan thought for a moment. "And if his clients are Russian, it might be a good idea for Harrison to stay missing for a long time. The Russians have a different sense of right and wrong than we do."

"Well, that's not exactly how the . . ." Cornwallis was showing a bit of emotion for an FBI agent.

Noonan cut her off, "That's how I read it. Now, I can't say *yes* or *no* about Mr. Harrison because the murder case is not my case. I'm just a hired gun. All I can do is tell Mr. Harrison Day Three"—he pointed at Harrison III—"when I see him, that someone is looking for him who says he is his son. Anything beyond that and you have to get Chief Standing Bear's permission."

"But you talked to my father two days ago," cut in Harrison III.

"So?"

"He's not in the mental facility anymore. He's gone."

Noonan was shocked. "How do you know that?"

"Chief Standing Bear got the call a few hours ago. He was asking us where my father was. Then he suggested we ask you. You were the last one to talk to him."

Then things got worse.

Harrison III tried to cut in, but Cornwallis stopped him with a hand on his upper arm. "As I told you before, Mr. Harrison, this is law-enforcement business first." Harrison III was not happy, but he stopped speaking midword. Then Cornwallis turned her attention to Noonan. "Making a long story short."

That's when Noonan cut her off, "No. Keep the long story long. We have quite a twisted collection of circumstances here."

Cornwallis sighed, looked at Harrison III, and then started anew, "Mr. Harrison, II, not III, has been on our radar in Pennsylvania for quite a while. He is an extremely clever lawyer, and most of his clients were midlevel banking people. For him this was both good and bad. It was good because he could keep his clients out of jail. It was bad because his clients usually ended up with no money to pay for his services. He has had plenty of clients but few who can pay."

"Doesn't sound odd to me." Noonan smiled knowingly. "If they don't go to jail, at least they end up paying for their crimes with a different coin."

Cornwallis gave a flicker of a smile, the most an FBI agent is allowed to do.

"As I am sure you are aware, Captain Noonan, when one is treading on the very edge of the law, there can be some slippage. Mr. Harrison II was involved in some suspected money-laundering enterprises involving Russian nationals when he came to the attention of Homeland Security. They asked for our assistance, and we provided that assistance. But we needed the cooperation of Mr. Harrison II."

"Let me guess. You sort of got it, and when you figured you'd been snookered, he was gone."

185

"Close enough to be accurate. There is money that has vaporized along with a number of the Russian nationals. Nothing we can prove but enough for us to open a bona fide investigation. We aren't here to arrest him, just to ask him some very pointed questions."

"Homeland Security! Why do you think I'm here?" Noonan retorted. "Now that we both know the political basics, where do we go from here?"

Harrison III tried to cut in, but Cornwallis stopped him short again. To him she said, "All in good time. Right now, there's no reason for a turf war." She looked at Noonan hesitantly.

Noonan agreed. "No reason for a turf war at all. I've got nothing. What do you know?"

"Nothing except that Harrison II popped up as being part of an investigation here. Chief Standing Bear looks at you as the lead, so that's why we're here."

Noonan smiled. "OK. Here's what I know. A man named Harrison"—he pointed at Harrison III—"who was not your father, checked into the Frank M. Canton Hotel here in Washakie. He paid for a room in cash. When hotel staff went to clean his room on the second morning, the place was drenched in blood. There was no body in the room and no sign a body had been dragged out."

"Where'd the body go?" Harrison III asked excitedly.

"Let's hear the rest of the story before we go asking questions," Cornwallis reprimanded Harrison III as if he were a small child.

"Sorry," Harrison III said to Noonan. "Go on."

Noonan didn't miss a beat. "Not a problem. There was plenty of blood in the room but, like I said, not outside the room as if a body had been dragged away. There was also no blood in the shower stall where a body might have been cut up or on the window in the room. There were some bloody footprints in the room but none outside."

"So how'd the body get out of the room?" Cornwallis was thinking like a cop.

"Good question. I don't have an answer."

"Where does my father come into this?" Harrison III was clearly not going to be left out of the conversation.

"No one is sure. Your father showed up the next day and asked for his room key. He said he was the Mr. Harrison who had checked into the room two days earlier."

"If he had been, he would have been killed," Harrison III said flatly. "What linked him to the murder?"

"Nothing," Noonan went on. "He had a weak alibi. He had been Casper at the time of the murder, and there is no evidence he had been in Washakie."

"So he just showed up in Washakie and asked for the same room as the other Harrison?"

"That's the size of it." Noonan raised his hands in helplessness. "He came walking into the hotel and asked for the key to his room. Said he was the Harrison who had paid for the room three days earlier. That's when the police became involved."

"Was he arrested?" Harrison III was quick to ask.

"Questioned, not arrested. There was no evidence against him. Add to that, he was not lucid. Schizophrenic would be a better term. Nothing he said was relevant to anything. The police chief and another officer took him to Casper."

"We know you visited him in Casper," Cornwallis interjected. "Did you find him lucid?"

"Nope. But I'm sure he was faking it."

"Why do you say that?" Cornwallis asked.

"Mr. Harrison impressed me as an actor rather than a patient. His fantasies were in complete sentences. Just as important, they were conventional. He probably spent some time on Google. No, he was lucid but kept trying to pass himself off as crazy. It was as though he pulled his role model from *One Flew over the Cuckoo's Nest* or *Captain Newman, M.D.* He's a very clever man." Then to Harrison III Noonan asked, "Does your father have any kind of an acting background?"

"Community theater for years," Harrison III said. "He was good but not great."

"Well, he was as good as he had to be for whatever reason he had. But now he's in the wind." Then to Cornwallis he said, "You might have made a very long trip for nothing at all."

CHAPTER 48

Alaskan humorist Warren Sitka famously noted that forgiving the unethical was like painting on an outgoing tide. Sandra Trucco had never heard of Warren Sitka, but she certainly understood the meaning of his words. In the years before she fled her roots on the Blackfoot Nation she had watched as large oil companies came into the Nation, drilled for oil, found oil, extracted profits, and left mountains of toxic debris. The only Blackfoot who profited were those not living in the Nation. They had taken the money and run.

Trucco had no illusions how the real world worked. The further up the food chain you were, the more money you could make and more disaster you would leave in your wake. Sin may follow its master like a dog, but when it came to money, the sin was empty pockets, and if you had $5 million, you could care less if people said you were unethical.

Trucco had seen an angle, and she took it. But she was not greedy. She knew what she could take, and that was her limit, an odd mentality for someone who had worked her way up the casino food chain in Las Vegas. Ironically, she found that truth in an old story she had been told as a child, the story of why the Blackfoot do not kill mice.

Once upon a time Bear and Beaver and Buffalo and Mouse gambled over a bone game to see who would be chief. Mouse won because he had some small, quick hands. But Mouse did not want to be chief. After Mouse won the bone game of who would be chief, Mouse stood in the center of the council of animals and said "'Listen, brothers—what is mine to keep is mine to give away. I am too small to be your chief, and I know it. I am not warlike. I want to live in peace with my wife and family. I know nothing of war. I get my living easily. I don't like to have enemies. I am going to give away my right to be chief." Thus did Mouse give the ruling of the world to man, and this is reason the Blackfoot never kill mice.

Trucco was too smart to demand more than her share of the pie. Trucco was not warlike. Trucco wanted to live in peace with the years she had left. And Trucco did not kill mice. Neither would Darby O'Reilly. When the tires of the 737 hit the tarmac in Nassau, neither of them was thinking about Wyoming or the Stupinigi Corporation or the Nimerigar or what was going to happen when the pigeons finally came home to roost.

CHAPTER 49

"Did you have a good time sightseeing Wyoming?" Washakie Chief of Police Leonard Standing Bear asked with a smile after Noonan broke free of Cornwallis and Harrison III.

"Only missed seeing a jackalope," Noonan responded.

"We don't see a lot them around here," Standing Bear responded with a smile. "Not in a long time."

Both men laughed.

Then Chief Standing Bear got serious. "I've got a lot of news for you, and none of it is good."

"This is not a business where you get a lot of good news."

"Tell me about it. I assume you already know Harrison Day Three is gone."

"That I know. Did he just walk out the door and disappear?"

"Basically, yes. Right after you talked to him. He waited a few hours and then checked himself out. It took his *loyer* a day to get the news. By then Harrison Day Three was long gone. We cannot put out an APB, so we're just stuck."

"No reason to put out an APB."

"You solved the case?" Standing Bear was hopeful.

"I'm putting the pieces together. It's a bit more complicated than the murder."

"Don't make me look bad in the paper," Standing Bear said with a smile. "Election's coming up."

"Someone else wants your job?" Noonan was humorously incredulous. Both men laughed.

Noonan smiled mischievously. "Rather than you telling me the bad news, let me guess."

"You are a devious soul, Heinz. OK. I'll play the game."

Noonan smiled. "OK. Here we go. "The bus-depot man told you the fire alarm had been set on by someone in the garage, not by the smoke detector."

"You are good."

"And the blood from the Frank M. Canton Hotel room is human but a mix of at least two people."

"You *are* as good as your reputation. Yes. There were two different blood signatures. We assume the perp was injured in the attack. Harrison Day Three had no injuries whatsoever, so that cleared him of the murder. We couldn't even hold him as a person of interest, so he's in the wind. How did you figure out there were two types of blood in the room?"

Noonan tapped his nose. "I've got a nose for crime."

"OK. What else you guess?"

"One of the names of the passengers on the tour bus was Sandra Trucco."

"Wow! How'd you know that?"

Again Noonan tapped his nose.

"Go on! I am impressed!"

"Sandra Trucco is missing, and Darby O'Reilly is on vacation never to return."

"I don't know that Trucco is missing, but I'll check. Darby's on vacation. Everyone knows that. Why do you think he's not coming back?"

Noonan tapped his nose.

"OK," Standing Bear said. "Let me guess. You're saving the best for last."

"You have been watching too many detective movies. You know, in the last five minutes all is revealed, and the bad guy gets his due."

"I do love happy endings," Standing Bear said wistfully.

"Well, this story will not necessarily have a *happy* ending. But it does have an ending."

"Good. I like it that way."

Noonan shook the forefinger of his right hand at Standing Bear humorously. "I'm a big fan of sharing good news. Why don't you tell Joshua Three Trees to be in your office the day after tomorrow? And the Bodacious brothers. I'll tell you what time. I have a few more invites to make."

"I *know*; you don't want to disappoint."

"*Anyone*," Noonan said. "Disappoint *anyone*. We've got a grammar Nazi on board."

"Ain't that the truth."

CHAPTER 50

It was not a meeting of happy campers. Neither of the men in the room were happy nor campers. They spoke English as a second language. Neither had ever heard of Chief of Detectives Heinz Noonan. Nor had they ever heard of Sandersonville, North Carolina. Neither of them had any desire to go to a flyspeck of civilization in the middle of nowhere. Nor had they ever had a desire to visit Wyoming. But the word had come down a pipeline. From the FBI of all people, the one agency that never said anything until an arrest was made. The FBI! Informing "those who were interested in what happened to the $20 million invested with Jerome McKinley Harrison II" should be in the Washakie Police Station in two days.

Wyoming?

But they did want to know what had happened to their $20 million.

So they did the best thing.

They sent their lawyer.

Washakie? Wyoming? What's in Washakie? What did it have to do with a construction project in the Lower Merion Township, and—most importantly—where was their legally earned $20 million?

CHAPTER 51

Noonan was sitting at the empty desk in the back of the Washakie Police Station talking with Harrison III and Cornwallis when Standing Bear came in with Joshua Three Trees and Harold Bodacious. The Bodacious brothers from Washakie were already present as was a man who refused to give his name. All the unknown man would say was he was "waiting for shoes to fall."

Harry and Sam Bodacious gave Harold Bodacious a cautious greeting.

A very cautious greeting.

"Now that we are all here," Standing Bear said with a smile, "I want to make everything crystal clear. You are all here because there is an active murder investigation here in Washakie, and to some extent you are all involved."

That created a firestorm.

The only one who was unconcerned was Harold Bodacious who was smugly leaning against a convenient wall with a sardonic smile on his face. Harrison III stood silently and Cornwallis was FBI calm, cool, and collected while she was clearly mentally "taking names and preparing to kick butt." At the other end of the excitement spectrum were Harry and Sam Bodacious who were acting like guilty shoplifters caught in the act.

Then things got worse.

194

Standing Bear introduced the unknown man, Leonoid Sikorski, who represented the Russian conglomerate of Grozny Inc. out of Philadelphia. If it would have been possible for white men to turn pale, Harry and Sam Bodacious would have done it.

Things were well out of hand when Noonan stood up from behind the desk, raised both his hands as if he were holding back a falling crate and said loudly—and pleasantly—"I'm so pleased you are all here." Then, when the hubbub had fallen to a soft roar, Noonan lowered his voice and pointed to a circle of chairs. "Why don't we have a little chat?"

Nonplussed, Harold Bodacious asked, "I'm assuming this is going to be like the end of some detective movie where all of the suspects are brought together for the truth to come out?"

"A clever observation, Harold. Yes and no. I'm just going to tell a little story, and anyone who wishes can add to it. If anyone wants to leave now, they are free to do so. E-x-c-e-p-t"—Noonan stretched out the word and while doing so pointed to Police Chief Standing Bear who was leaning against the back wall by the exit door with a sheaf of folded papers—"anyone who does leave early, well, Chief Standing Bear might have a piece of paper for them." Chief Standing Bear fanned a sheaf of folded sheets of paper in his left hand. (He was a southpaw.)

"Well, you know, we had nothing whatsoever to do with any murder," cut in Sam Bodacious while his brother Harry did a chicken-head-nodding routine.

"Will you just shut up?" snapped Harold Bodacious, uncharacteristically short. "Let's just get this over with."

Sam and Harry kept mumbling, but it was so low no one cared.

Noonan gave an avuncular smile as he looked around the room. "There's no reason for anyone to be upset"—he smiled—"yet." After a pause, he continued, "I'm just telling you a story. Feel free to correct me if I get something wrong."

Now there was dead silence.

"Well," said Noonan with a smile. "So far I'm correct." Then he pointed to Harrison III and Cornwallis. "None of you"—he then pointed in a half circle to the chairs—"have asked about these individuals, so let me introduce them." He pointed at Harrison III first. "This is Jerome

McKinley Harrison III. He is the son of Jerome McKinley Harrison II, of course. Jerome McKinley Harrison II is the second Mr. Harrison who arrived at the Frank M. Canton Hotel and asked for his room key, the key to the room soaked in blood. Jerome McKinley Harrison II won't be here, alas, because he is missing in action, so to speak. He checked out of the psychiatric facility in Casper several days ago and has not been seen since."

There was dead silence in the room.

Pointing at Cornwallis, Noonan added, "And this is Special Agent Jennifer Cornwallis from the Philadelphia FBI. It seems that Jerome McKinley Harrison II has been a rather bad boy. He had been given twenty million dollars." Noonan smiled craftily. Then he added softly, "In cash." He pointed to Leonid Sikorski of the Russian conglomerate of Grozny Inc. "The FBI was interested in the source of that twenty million dollars and was pressuring their lawyer, Jerome McKinley Harrison II for its source. Then"—Noonan made a pooofffiiinngg motion with his right hand in the air—"Jerome McKinley Harrison II disappeared."

Sikorski stood up and started to say something, but Noonan silenced him with a wave of his hand. To Sikorski, specifically, Noonan added, "FBI Agent Cornwallis is still looking for Jerome McKinley Harrison II, and I must assume she continues to be interested in the source of that twenty million dollars. I'm sure she will have some questions for you after this little tête-à-tête."

Sikorski immediately sat down—quietly.

Noonan looked at Harrison III and Cornwallis and added, "Since the two of you do not know these gentlemen, allow me to introduce them. The tall man is Joshua Three Trees who is the spokesman for the Nimerigar Natives."

"CEO," cut in Three Trees. "We officially formed a corporation three days ago. We are now a corporation."

"My apologies," Noonan quickly added. "I did not know that had happened." Then turning to Cornwallis, he said, "CEO Joshua Three Trees of the now incorporated Nimerigar Native operation. The gentleman still standing and leaning against the far wall is Harold Bodacious, the attorney for an Italian corporation."

At that moment, Harold Bodacious cut Noonan off, "That's no longer the case, Heinz, er, Captain Noonan. At the same meeting where the Nimerigar Native Corporation was formed, the Stupinigi Corporation transferred all its assets to the Nimerigar Native Corporation. As the Stupinigi Corporation no longer exists, I am without that client."

"I see," Noonan looked stoic. "However, as of an hour ago, no transfer of assets or corporation papers had been filed with the State of Wyoming, so even though there is a hiatus, you have been invited here as a transitioning representative of the Stupinigi Corporation."

"The paperwork has been filed and accepted by the State of Wyoming," Harold Bodacious said stoically. "The hiatus, to use your term, has no legal standing."

"A fine point. I'm just doing my due diligence," said Noonan. "Feel free to go. But," he stated cagily, "be sure to check with Chief Standing Bear to make certain there are no legal complications."

Chief Standing Bear made a show of looking through the fan of folded papers in his mighty paw.

"I love a good story," Harold Bodacious said cockily. "I've have nothing better to do."

"Fine," Noonan said and then turned to Cornwallis. "There two gentlemen are Sam and Harry Bodacious, distantly related to Harold, the lawyer"—Noonan pointed to Harold Bodacious. "The Bodacious brothers were robbed at gunpoint here in Washakie. Harry is a coin dealer and Sam is a jeweler."

Noonan put on a sad face. "There are two participants missing, I must add. Darby O'Reilly from the State of Wyoming is on vacation, and his girlfriend, Sandra Trucco, is not in Bridger. She did not show up at work three days ago and has not been heard from since. She is not at her home and told no one she was leaving town. We assume she is with her boyfriend because"—he looked at Cornwallis—"through the services of the FBI, we know that the two of them took a flight out of Denver for Nassau."

"That's in the Cayman Islands, isn't it?" asked Sam Bodacious hopefully.

"Bahamas," corrected Harold Bodacious. "You should never have dropped out of high school, Sam."

"Be that as it may," Noonan said quickly to keep the presentation on track, "both Darby O'Reilly and Sandra Trucco are missing."

"As is my father," cut in Harrison III.

"True," Noonan added. "Your father is still missing. Now, to continue my story, in the early 1970s the US government cut a deal with the Alaska Natives. To stop them from taking what became the Trans-Alaska Pipeline to court, the Natives were given almost a billion dollars in cash and more than forty million acres of land."

"What does Alaska have to do with Wyoming?" cut in Harry Bodacious.

"All will be made clear quickly," Noonan replied. "Those Natives who were actually living in Alaska at the time split up the more than forty million acres of land and the money. All one billion dollars of it was divided among all Alaska Natives whether they were living in Alaska or not."

"What kind of Alaska Natives weren't living in Alaska? Why do you know so much about Alaska, and who cares?" Sam Bodacious was showing his lack of intelligence grandly.

"A fair question," Noonan said, nonplussed. "Alaska Natives are just like everyone else. They join the military and leave the state. They get married and leave the state. They go to school out of state. They get offered a good paying job out of the state. It doesn't matter why they left Alaska. Only that when the land was divided, they were not going to get any land. I know so much about Alaska, by the way, because my wife is Alaskan. One of those Alaskans who left the state to get a better job and get married. What does this have to do with Wyoming? Listen and learn."

Harry was about to say something but stopped short of saying it.

Noonan continued. "Those Alaska Natives outside of Alaska formed what is known as the 13th Corporation. That's because there were twelve Native corporations in the state. The 13th Corporation included Alaska Natives of all ethnic varieties. The 13th Corporation was the seed of the Nimerigar for Nathaniel Three Trees"—Noonan looked at Harrison III and Cornwallis—"the father of Joshua." He finished by pointing at Joshua Three Trees. Then he turned back to the group.

"If the Alaska Natives could form a corporation of many ethnic strains, so could he. That was the seed when he formed the Nimerigar from the locals who were at least one-fourth Native. That satisfied Affirmative

Action requirements for Native blood. But a collection of people calling themselves Natives didn't make a dime, so Nathaniel went after land. You cannot make money anywhere unless you have land. Nathaniel fought the Washington bureaucracy for land for the Nimerigar. Native land, let me quickly add. Because if you have Native land, you are not subject to state laws—like gambling restrictions."

"We all know this, so why are we rehashing history?" Sam finally had the backbone to make a statement.

"Because at least three people in the room have never heard of Nimerigar," Noonan said pointing his finger at Cornwallis, Sikorski, and Harrison III one at a time.

Noonan continued, this time looking from Cornwallis to Sikorski to Harrison III as if he were just talking to them. "Land in Wyoming has no value unless it has access, water, and power. The Nimerigar had fifty thousand acres of land, about twenty miles by fifteen miles, but it was twenty-five miles from the interstate and had no water and no power. And here is where the story gets complicated."

The room was dead silent.

"What I believe but cannot *prove*"—Noonan accented the word *prove*—"is that Jerome McKinley Harrison II, a lawyer from Philadelphia, who was also a Vietnam buddy of Nathaniel Three Trees, set a scheme in motion. He took the twenty million dollars from Grozny Inc., the Russians, and formed a phantom corporation in Italy, Stupinigi. The Stupinigi Corporation had the required five corporate officers to be legal in Italy, three of them Italian. But two them did not exist. One of the two American officers was dead; now both are. And the corporation was run out of a mailbox in Torino."

"So it was shell," cut in Cornwallis.

"Absolutely," Noonan replied. "It was a way to wash money." He looked at Sikorski, "your company's money."

Sikorski started to mouth something that appeared to be "that son of a . . ."

"But money in a foreign corporation needed to make money in Wyoming. What the Stupinigi Corporation had to do was get the title to critical acres of land around the Nimerigar property. Now things get murky. It was able to buy the old Laramie Consolidate Syndicate lands for under ten thousand dollars. That was the price on the books for the property at the land office of the State of Wyoming. That's where I believe—but cannot prove—that Darby O'Reilly first came in contact with both the Nimerigar and the Stupinigi Corporation. The lands of the Laramie Consolidate Syndicate were important because its property had included a railroad spur, now defunct, that ended a few miles from the Wyoming power-transmission web. Once the Stupinigi Corporation had all the land between the Nimerigar property and the power grid, the planned casino on Nimerigar property would have unending cheap power. And"—Noonan held up his finger as Harold Bodacious was about to say something—"the New York Photovoltaic Company was poised to build on Nimerigar land. And why not? The land would have been free, and a transmission corridor to the statewide power grid was assured."

Now Harold Bodacious cut in, "But the Stupinigi Corporation did not own those final three miles."

"They didn't have to own them," said Noonan. "Darby O'Reilly, representing the State of Wyoming, had already sold them to Sandra Trucco. Trucco paid with a cashier's check from her personal savings. The raw land was incredibly cheap because it was the Badlands"—Noonan paused—"and the land was sold three years ago. What Trucco got for the land when she sold it to the Stupinigi Corporation is unknown, but it's hard to believe she did not make a killing. Even better, because Darby O'Reilly worked for the State of Wyoming in the office that made the sale, it made the sale of the land to the Stupinigi through Trucco an arm's length transaction for everyone."

"OK, so that's how the power was going to be provided to the casino," Harrison III said. "But you said the Indian group, the Nim . . ."

"Nimerigar," snapped Three Trees. "Nimerigar. Get it right."

"Right," said Harrison III. "But they still needed water. Where was that going to come from?"

"Buckle Bunny Lake in Bridger."

"There was public land for sale all the way to the lake?" Harrison III was incredulous.

"Harold," Noonan said as he looked at Harold Bodacious, "perhaps you can explain."

"Now I know why I was invited," Harold snapped. "OK, to continue the story offered by Captain Noonan, one hundred percent of the land around Buckle Bunny Lake and back, say six miles, is private. Where possible, title to a corridor for a water-transportation pipeline was negotiated with the landowners. The Stupinigi . . ."

Noonan cut him off, "Actually, what you have heard is not completely true. While there were many individual landowners, they were all part of one large trust, the Bodacious Trust. Thus, negotiating the sale of the corridor only meant dealing with one lawyer, Harold Bodacious, who was also the lawyer for the Bodacious Trust."

"An entirely legal representation," cut in Harold. "It was approved by the board of directors of the Bodacious Trust."

"True," said Noonan. "But according to the corporate papers, the Bodacious Trust is composed of you, your wife, your two sons, and your father. I understand both your father and your wife have passed along. Is that accurate?"

"Unfortunately, that is true. But the board, as a body, still approved the sale."

"True or not, the sale was legal. But that left a lot of land to cover. It is a long way from Buckle Bunny Lake to the Nimerigar property. The Stupinigi Corporation"—Noonan pointed at Harold—"represented by Harold here, negotiated with both the Bureau of Land Management and the State of Wyoming for public lands. That took place quickly and easily because no one was buying rattlesnake-country land. But that left a dozen plots of land that were private. Without a corridor across those lands there would be no water from Buckle Bunny Lake."

At this point, Noonan stopped talking and pulled out a massive manila file. "Land status in Wyoming is like land status everywhere: it is a rat's nest of documents, liens, conveyances, easements, leases, sales, mining claims, bankruptcy filings, and transfers." He shook the file. "When I finally figured out that the key to the murder was land, I went to the land records. Which was a mistake. The key to the murder was not the land records but historic corporation records. You see," he said to no one in particular, "you only own land if you have the paperwork to prove it. And a lot of that paperwork is convoluted—the reason you buy title insurance when you buy land. By using the Google Map overview, I was able to isolate the Nimerigar land and the Stupinigi Land and the Bodacious land. I then drew a straight line from Buckle Bunny Lake to the Nimerigar Land. But that straight line was odd because it ran straight across a dozen small pieces of property. Then I used the just-introduced land-computerization program of the State of Wyoming and isolated those dozen properties. I then went back to see who owned those properties. I was quite surprised to find that all of the land that composed what is now the corridor from Buckle Bunny Lake across those lands had been deeded to three different corporations more than fifty years ago. And those corporations, which went defunct, deeded just the corridor acres to other corporations, which also went defunct—but not before deeding the land to yet other corporation, which also went defunct, until the Stupinigi Corporation ended up with the corridor."

"You would have a hard time proving that in a court of law," Harold Bodacious cut in. "The boards of directors of those corporations are long gone. Not to mention their corporate papers. If those corporate papers exist at all."

"True," said Noonan. "Even if any one of the alleged sales was found to be false, the subsequent sales would be legal. So the title-insurance company would have to make good on the false claim."

"A sad situation," said Harold Bodacious wolfishly.

"True. But I was not brought here to look at land issues but a murder."

"So we're finally getting to the murder?" Sam Bodacious seemed relieved.

"Absolutely," Noonan said smiling. "But we have to finish with the land. What I suggest happened is that a lawyer drew up a dozen legal bills of sales on old paper with ancient ink, making the land sales look authentic. It would not have been hard. All the lawyer had to have was a list of defunct corporations," Noonan said, jiggling the manila folder, "like these, which you can get from the Wyoming archives. But for the scheme to work, the lawyer would have had to gotten the fraudulent documents into the Wyoming Land filing system in the right spot. That would not be hard by someone who knew the system."

"Darby O'Reilly," said Cornwallis excitedly.

"Most likely," Noonan replied. "But he is not here to defend himself."

"Not yet," said Cornwallis.

"He might not ever come back," Noonan said. "Continuing on, this land person had two problems. First, he—or she—had to go through reams of already-filed documents over the past century to find the exact spot to put in each document. And not just in one land office, four: three counties and the state-land office in Cheyenne. If that person worked in Cheyenne in the land office, that would not be a problem in Cheyenne. But it would be a problem in the county courthouses. The documents had to be placed perfectly. Once they were, no one would know about the land transfers for years. If ever. Those pieces of property from where the Buckle Bunny Lake water would be transferred does not have residents. It is investment property. It is quite possible no one would ever know the corridor had been deeded. And now that the Stupinigi Corporation no longer exists, there is another defunct corporation to deal with."

Harold Bodacious was about say something but Noonan cut him off.

"For that person in the Wyoming Land Office, the computerization of land records was both a blessing and a curse. As a blessing it would cement the fraudulent land records into the land history of the state. It was a curse because, I believe, the person in the Wyoming Land Office had not had the opportunity to spend the time—alone, let me quickly add—to get the fraudulent documents into the right file in the right place in the right county courthouse."

Noonan paused for a moment and then continued, "Thus the three robberies. The three robberies were not designed to steal anything, just to draw away people who worked in the county courthouse. The gun being spotted near the school in Bridger by, of all people, Sandra Trucco, was near a school. That drew the police to the school. More importantly, it drew away parents with children who worked in the county courthouse. That left Darby O'Reilly alone in the county courthouse in Bridger. In Washakie, a smoking bus tripped the fire alarm in the bus station. That drew away the insurance agent who was working part time in the county courthouse. One of the passengers on that bus was Sandra Trucco. Her name popped up on the state troopers' blockade list. I'm guessing she injected some liquid in the hot exhaust pipe of the bus. The liquid turned to blue smoke. Then she hit the fire alarm. That cleared out the bus terminal and drew the insurance woman out of the courthouse, giving Darby O'Reilly who was in the courthouse time to place the critical land documents. In Colter, Darby O'Reilly was in the county courthouse alone over the Fourth of July. That gave him all day to place the documents."

"Well," snapped Sam desperately, "what about the murder!"

"There never was one," responded Noonan. "It was a distraction. The same for the robberies. The murder and the robberies were to give the land person, probably Darby O'Reilly, time to make the land transfers. I am sure that a Jerome Harrison"—Noonan looked at Harrison III—"your father, got a friend to check into the Frank M. Canton Hotel. He spent one night, and the room was cleaned with no problem. On the second night, someone with access to blood like Sandra Trucco, who worked at the Bridger Hospital, mucked the place with blood. Then the other Harrison, your father"—he indicated Harrison III—"showed up after spending a few days in a homeless shelter in Casper. That gave him an alibi. He feigned insanity, and the Washakie police had to take him to the psychiatric facility in Casper. That cut down the number of police in town."

"But how does that time with the robberies?" Sam Bodacious asked, hopeful he could pull the conversation sideways.

"They never happened either."

"No way," snapped Harry. "We've got a robbery on a security camera."

"You have it on a baby cam. There is no time and date stamp. I suspect it was filmed long before the robbery ever took place. What bothered me was how the robbers could disappear. There were roadblocks and searches and nothing. So where were the robbers hiding? In fact, there were no robbers. The witness in Bridger was Sandra Trucco. And the victims were a pair of Bodacious brothers." Noonan looked at Harold. "Some of your relatives. Any chance they are part of the Bodacious Trust?"

Harold said nothing.

"And the robbery was a burglary. There were no security alarms, so the alleged burglary could have happened the night before. No one knows. Disappearing in Colter during the Fourth of July was easy. But to make the robberies look real, someone had to come up with proof. Thus the baby cam. I'm betting the robbery was filmed weeks before, and then, just as the bus in the garage began smoking, the police station was called. Now, in a single afternoon, you had Chief Standing Bear and another officer out of town with Harrison, cops at two burglaries, and the fire alarm. The fire alarm also drew the insurance agent out of the county courthouse. That gave the Wyoming land person all the time he—or she—needed to make the title transfer."

There was a silence for a moment. Finally Harold said, "Well, this is all well and good, but I don't see you have any proof of anything. I don't see that a crime has been committed anywhere."

"Maybe," said Noonan. Then he looked around the room. "I've had my say. What happens next depends on the FBI"—he pointed to Cornwallis—"and the State of Wyoming." He smiled beatifically. "I thank you for your time and patience."

Everyone stood up and began leaving when Noonan waved Harry Bodacious and Three Trees over. "Sam," Noonan said in an interesting tone, "when I asked you about the robbers, you said the man was 'six feet two and a half inches tall.' That's a pretty precise measurement. Most people would have said over six feet or six foot two or three inches. Odd."

"Well, I guess I was being precise."

"You saw him, so you should know. I mean, you were on the baby cam, so you were eyeball to eyeball with him."

"Yeaaah."

"I estimate Jerome McKinley Harrison II was about six foot two or three. You ever meet him?"

"Nnnnooo."

"Odd. Then there was the woman everyone was reporting. But she was only on camera once. The baby cam. She looked about the same size as Sandra Trucco. You ever meet Sandra Trucco?"

"Nnnnooo."

"Odd. You can go now. Joshua!"

Three Trees was sullen.

Noonan smiled. "In my business I get sent to places I have never even thought about going. The downside is that no matter where I go, I am an

205

outsider. I have to discover what everyone else has known for years. The upside is I get to learn the history of the area. History is not the story of the past; it's the study of the future. You find clues in the past to help you in the future. Far too many people walk around with the attitude that 'nothing ever happens here, so I live in a dull place.' Well, if you do not know where you have been, you do not know where you are going."

"Oh, I know where we've been," snapped Three Trees for the first time. "You white men came, slaughtered, stole, and occupied the land. Left us to starve."

"Partially true," Noonan said. "There's been a lot of coming, slaughtering, and stealing in all parts of the world by all kinds of people over the past fifteen thousand years. But we are not here to talk about that."

Three Trees snorted.

"Joshua, I want to tell you a little story. A Wyoming story. It's one of those tidbits of local history you pick up when you actually spend time learning local history. In 1876, two wily old Wyoming prospectors came up with a brilliant scheme. They gathered what money they had and went to Amsterdam where they bought the chips and chards of the diamond industry and brought the pieces to Wyoming where they salted a field near Pulpit Rock, a very impressive precipice, I must add. Then the prospector began looking for investors in this lucrative find. To prove the diamond find was real, they got investors to agree to come to the site blindfolded. Once on the field, the investors were free to scramble around and *find* valuable gemstones. They got investors as far away as San Francisco and New York and their rubes included the Rothschild family, Louis Tiffany, and Horace Greeley. When the prospectors got their money, they scampered away.

The point here is that investors should have known better. According to the assay report of the find, if *assay* is the correct term to use for precious stones, it was impossible to find a location on earth where diamonds, oriental rubies, garnets, spinels, sapphires, emeralds, and amethysts all existed together—with the exception of a precious-gem operation."

"There's a point to this story," growled Three Trees.

"Sure is," replied Noonan. "Everything that has happened with regard to the two Harrisons and the three robberies has been a con. I'm leaving town, but you've got to stay. You have to weather the investigations by the feds and the state. It is not going to be pleasant. Then there are the Russians. They are different folk when it comes to money. They don't use the courts. They'll find Jerome McKinley Harrison II. They are very good at finding people. You, they don't have to look very far to find."

Three Trees left the room with an ashen face.

Noonan was putting his paperwork back in his briefcase when Standing Bear came from the back of the room. "Joshua did not look like a happy camper."

"If I were him, I would not be a happy camper."

"A fine presentation. As good as I have ever seen."

"When you get to be my age, you will be just as good as I was today. Maybe even better."

"You are a master, Heinz. I particularly like the power of paper," he fanned the folded slips of paper.

"Illusion, Leonard. It's not what's on the paper that counts. It's what people *think* is on the paper."

Standing Bear unfolded one of the sheets. It was blank. "Magic! It's gone from a subpoena to a yet-to-be-paper-airplane."

"Everything in life is a yet-to-be, Leonard. That's why we get up every morning. Every morning is an opportunity with places to go, people to see, things to do, mistakes to make."

CHAPTER 52

There is an old Caribbean expression that is universal: "A no wantin tongue mek cattle can't talk." It translates into English as "It's sometimes wisest to keep one's mouth shut." It was an expression Sandra Trucco and Darby O'Reilly took seriously.

Very seriously.

That was because both had everything to lose. If there was anything Trucco knew too well, it was poverty. She had been born into it and been forced to live it. Then she had gone to Las Vegas and watched billions in cash flood around her, and she had ended up as an administrative assistant in a small town in the Badlands. Worse, she had watched as large corporations rolled over the poor as if they did not exist. The Blackfoot nation had three thousand square miles of nothing, a landmass twice the size of Delaware. Then, when the oil companies came to drill, the Blackfoot people got nothing.

Not a dime.

That was not going to happen to her. The only thing she wanted to remember of her Blackfoot Nation days was not to kill mice.

Darby O'Reilly had been scorched by different lettering from the same branding iron. He had come from a family of bureaucrats in a state that did not honor them. He had the same job as his father and grandfather, and it was on the chopping block. He had never had a plan B. Neither had his father nor his grandfather. It wasn't that they knew better or wanted better. What they had was adequate. His grandfather had been lucky to have a job during the Depression, and his father had needed the job with a young wife and child. Darby had neither. When it became clear to him plan A was closing out, he had a choice: be a Luddite or run with the wind.

The stars had aligned on the windswept plains of Wyoming, and both Trucco and O'Reilly saw the opportunity. Both had seen the big money rush by their home and hearth with nary a dime left on the welcome mat. So they played the game. They weren't greedy; they were frugal. They didn't need much, and the millions they had would last their lifetime.

As long as they stayed small and quiet and beyond the two-hundred-mile limit, all would be well for two elderly retirees who personified the Caribbean adage "A no wantin tongue mek cattle can't talk."

Jerome McKinley Harrison II was going to have a harder time of it.

EPILOGUE

"Where are you going from here?" Standing Bear asked Noonan through the open driver's side window of the rented car.

"Who knows," Noonan said wistfully. "I started out as a cop on a beat and ended up on the coast. But I don't spend a lot of time there. I'm called all over."

"If you ever come back this way, you be sure to stop in." Noonan turned the ignition key and the ancient wreck jolted alive. Standing Bear smiled. "Next time get a real car, not a rental wreck."

"All part of the budgeting process. By the way"—Noonan turned sideways and opened his briefcase and pulled out a manila envelope—"can you deliver something for me?"

"Sure. What is it?"

Noonan handed Standing Bear an 8½" × 11" manila envelope. "Seems I neglected to turn this over to the FBI."

Standing Bear gave Noonan a "get real" look. "Do I want to know what's in here?"

"They are all public documents, so you can certainly look. While I was looking through the corporation index provided by Wyoming's very efficient historical archivists, I noticed some items that might need investigation."

"Uh-huh," said Standing Bear waiting for a shoe to drop.

"It seems to me—but I'm not an expert in the matter—that there are some loose ends."

"Uh-huh."

"When the Stupinigi Corporation was absorbed by the Nimerigar, the Stupinigi Corporation went defunct. Its paperwork led back to the equivalent of a post-office box in Torino, Italy. Two of the directors are from Wyoming, both of them dead: Nathaniel Three Trees who just died and his daughter who was dead at the time; she was supposedly a director. Then there was a Martini and a Rossi, which, in Italian, is a joke. Martini & Rossi is a brand of vermouth. Even if there really were a Martini and a Rossi on the board of directors, they will be impossible to find. The name *Martini* in Italy is like *Smith* in America, and the name *Rossi* is like *Jones*. All the corporation papers have signed documents of Giuseppe Martini and Geraldo Rossi with a post-office address."

"Uh-huh."

Noonan smiled and tapped the manila envelope in Standing Bear's hand. "But the last name on the corporation paperwork is Lorenzo Furbo. *Furbo*, in the local dialect of Torino, Piedmontese, translates as clever. Like a fox. And there is no Lorenzo Furbo in the Torino phonebook or on Google."

"Uh-huh."

"So, I thought, well, if there isn't a Furbo in Torino, could there be one in Wyoming? And guess what?"

"Let me guess," Standing Bear cut in. "You found one."

"Actually, yes. But it was a convoluted process. Remember, the Stupinigi Corporation bought a lot of land in this area."

"With Russian money."

"Probably. But that's half the point. While we were concentrating on the Nimerigar and the FBI was concentrating on finding Harrison Day Three, no one was looking beyond the obvious."

"And the obvious was?"

"That Harrison Day Three was a slippery, disreputable individual."

"Oh?"

"How do I know? I don't. Here's what I'm guessing. About three years ago, when this whole scheme was being born, Harrison Day Three, who we now know was the Philadelphia lawyer, gave Darby O'Reilly a list of target properties. From what we know now, it was a laundry list of state and private lands. For those private lands, O'Reilly had to mock up historically accurate title deeds and insert them in the appropriate county-land-record collections."

"Before the computerization was complete, yes, I know that." Standing Bear was clearly confused.

"True. But not state land. See, we know the scam involved transferring fake land titles to the defunct companies that then, on paper, transferred the land to the Stupinigi Corporation, which then became property of the Nimerigar. That made it a problem for the title companies, not Nimerigar. They could say they bought the land legally."

"And the Stupinigi could say the same thing. If, that is, any of the corporate directors are ever asked"—Standing Bear took a deep breath—"which will never happen because the company no longer exists, and Joshua Three Trees will plead ignorance."

"Correct. But you see, Leonard, that was the beauty of this entire operation. We spent all our time looking at the *private* land that was transferred."

"What other land is there? It can't be federal land. The BLM people are straight as arrows."

"State land, Leonard; state land. The scheme we focused on was corridor land. When state land was needed, O'Reilly just deeded it over. No muss, no fuss. He had the power to do it. So he did. He was the entire land department. Who was going to question him?"

"No one. What's your point?"

"The point is that O'Reilly conveyed a lot of land that was not corridor land. It was raw land, but it was land."

"OK. To whom did he convey the land?"

"To Lorenzo Furbo."

"That makes no sense. Lorenzo Furbo does not exist. O'Reilly was transferring land to a person who did not exist, who could never take ownership of land?"

"That's what made it so clever. Remember I told you I found Lorenzo Furbo in Wyoming?"

212

Standing Bear rolled his eyes. Another shoe was about to drop. "I'll bite. Where did you find Lorenzo Furbo?"

"Here in Washakie."

"No way!"

"Way! Some of the State of Wyoming land that O'Reilly transferred to the Stupinigi Corporation was then transferred to Lorenzo Furbo. I'm betting O'Reilly did those land transfers as well."

"But that makes no sense," Standing Bear said. "Even if Harrison II or Furbo had land in his own name, he can't get it because he's on the run."

"That's what I thought. Then I saw that the land had been transferred again. See, Lorenzo Furbo, on paper, died."

"Died?"

"Yes, in Italy. A death certificate was issued in Torino."

"Then who gets the property?"

"I'm glad you asked. Not only was the property deeded to Lorenzo Furbo, Lorenzo Furbo also filed a probate will. Here in Washakie. In the event of Lorenzo Furbo's death, his property goes to . . ."

"Let me guess," snapped Standing Bear. "His son."

"Half right. Two men inherited the property: Joshua Three Trees and Jerome McKinley Harrison III."

Noonan paused for a breath. "The reason the supposed murder took place in Washakie was because O'Reilly needed *a lot* of time in the county courthouse. Not only did he have to plant the fraudulent land deeds, he had to file the land transfers to Lorenzo Furbo *and then* file the death certificate of Lorenzo Furbo and the probate paperwork. He needed law enforcement out of town, and he needed the county courthouse empty long enough to file all the documents. It was just a matter of the right ink stamps. He knew where all the stamps were located and used them. The supposed murder pulled two cops out of six out of Washakie, and the fire alarm on the bus and the robberies kept the rest of the department busy. It gave O'Reilly the time he needed."

"Well planned, I must say."

"Then it gets better. Where do you think the land Harrison and Three Trees inherited is?"

"If it's going be worth anything, it's along what used to be the Stupinigi Corporation and Nimerigar land border. I'm guessing near where the roadway meets Nimerigar property."

"You are one smart cop."

"Which explains why Harrison III showed up with the FBI agent. I thought it was strange he'd be here for what basically was a missing-person case."

"You're a good cop. You can smell a rat." Noonan smiled.

"Too late."

"Not yet. I figure Harrison III knew his father was going to be in the wind. With his father gone, the link between father and land was severed. The death certificate did that. So he had to be here to take possession of the land. He wasn't here to find his dad; he was here to take care of the probate."

"So where does that leave us?"

"Not us, Leonard, you. I'm on my way back to Sandersonville. But, at the very least, a smart man like you just might be able to—at the very least—throw a monkey wrench into the gears. Me, I'm looking forward to a week on the beach."

Just then Noonan's beast of Satan jiggled in his breast pocket. "Oh no!" he said, and he dragged the pestilential monster from his pocket. "Evil has come back to life."

Standing Bear put his hand on Noonan's arm. "Don't answer it. Just tell whoever is calling that there's no reception between Washakie and the civilized world. No one is going to doubt that."

"Sage advice from a young man." Then he rolled up the car window and rolled out onto the rural highway and headed out across the badlands.